DEAD TO RITES

DEAD TO RITES

by Sylvia Angus

CROWN PUBLISHERS, INC.,
New York

Printed in the United States of America
Published simultaneously in Canada by
General Publishing Company Limited

Book Design: Huguette Franco

Library of Congress Cataloging in Publication Data

Angus, Sylvia.
Dead to rites.

I. Title
PZ4 . A613Dd   [PS3551.N5]   813' . 5'4   78–15429
ISBN 0–517–53435–5

Second Printing, December, 1978

DEAD TO RITES

1

MRS. WAGSTAFF'S OBOE VOICE ACHIEVED PENETRATION
by piercing below rather than above the din of her fellow bus pas-
sengers.

"This vehicle is *unsanitary,*" she said, and instantly the dusty seat
she was observing from black, basilisk eyes looked not merely tar-
nished but diseased, leprous. There was a silence. Two ladies with
blue-waved hair stopped lowering themselves into their seats, tottered erect, and looked beneath them in dismay.

The driver looked at Mrs. Wagstaff's formidable silhouette and let
out a thin yelp of pain. He had been through a good deal on this
trip with the lady. He had learned a lot, too. Without comment or
discussion, he pulled out a rag, went back, and, under a battery of
critical, housewifely eyes, wiped off a dozen seats.

"A great improvement," Mrs. Wagstaff fluted graciously. Her
smile was sudden and surprising. There was a humorous quirk to
her broad mouth, which went oddly with her bulk and the continu-
ous demands of her dignity. The driver grinned, rubbed a dirty
hand across his chin, and went back up front, appeased.

"I don't know how you do it," little Mrs. Crummit fluttered, sitting down at last. Mrs. Crummit would obviously have sat on nails all the way to Chichén Itzá rather than complain.

"You must never accept shoddiness." Mrs. Wagstaff was firm. "To do so just creates more. Voicing dissatisfaction is necessary to improve the quality of life." She looked at poor Mrs. Crummit a moment as the bus began to move and saw that that rule of life was clearly wasted on her. "Never mind," she said kindly. "Isn't it a lovely day?"

A chorus of assent arose. It *was* a lovely day. Again. It had been a lovely day now for the entire ten days of their trip. Mrs. Wagstaff looked out, nodded her great head with Olympian approval, and turned to adjust her bag. It was, as always, in need of attention. Roughly the size of a sailor's gunny sack, it had innumerable ingenious pockets, but only a drawstring top. As a result, whatever was in the pockets slid out whenever the bag was put down sideways, or fell over. Mrs. Wagstaff picked up off the seat, and replaced, her paperback calorie counter, a small fold-up umbrella, a black-and-white child's copybook, and a large bottle of water-purification tablets. Professor Michelson, in the seat ahead, leaned down, picked up her flashlight, and returned it with round, brown eyes rolling impiously toward heaven. It had been a long ten days.

Across the aisle, Mr. Cartwright adjusted his wife's chair with a metallic crash which made her wince. Her head shook and nodded like a windup toy, on and on. The poor creature, paralyzed by a stroke, had only a few possible motions. She could move her head a little, and her left hand. She couldn't speak, but sometimes a harsh cry came from one side of her mouth. Mr. Cartwright was a saint to take her about as he did, just to distract her. A nice-looking man like that. What a disaster for him! They were all agreed on his sanctity. All except Barbara, of course. Barbara treated him with a teasing amusement that Mrs. Harvey Gibson found quite disgusting in a girl young enough to be his daughter. Whenever she looked at Barbara, Mrs. Gibson's wattles shook indignantly. But that, Mrs. Wagstaff thought, was because Barbara was so far from wattles as yet. She was slim, honey blonde, with an incredibly tiny waist, and it seemed the ultimate insult to all the other ladies on the bus that she should also be tanned the color of a peach and have green eyes. A tour bus was no place for her, of course, certainly not *this* one, where the average age was about fifty-five. She and her tall, plain cousin Susan were the only young people in the group . . . and Susan hardly counted. Certainly she didn't count herself, Mrs. Wagstaff thought disapprovingly. She was one of those girls who *might* look like something if she shook her hair loose and batted her eyes a bit . . . but such an idea had clearly never struck her. The only other young person on the bus was José Bunuelos, the tour guide. He was a charming, perhaps too intense young man . . . and he knew all about what elderly ladies liked. His dark eyes could be melting, and his strong, brown arm was always ready to assist them over the smallest curbstones. And he knew everything, it seemed, from the burial customs of the Chihuahuas to the exact height—in feet or meters—of the Guadalajara cathedral. He knew, in fact, almost as much as Mrs. Wagstaff did.

The big bus pulled out of its place in front of the hotel, away from the cool interior patio—it was a first-class tour—away from the man selling lottery tickets on the sidewalk and the woman with an armful of cotton hammocks stretched yearningly after them.

"Well, so much for Mérida!" said Mrs. Gibson with satisfaction. She had pronounced the same epitaph for each place they had rolled out of, as though she were running a pencil through a laundry list.

"It was a lovely city, didn't you think?" asked Mrs. Crummit anxiously. It was the first trip she had ever taken further from home than Pocatello, Idaho, and she did want every place she saw to be special. At every stop she sent a giant postcard to her daughter telling her how *that* stop was special.

"Pretty dead, if you ask me," said Barbara airily.

"The church was beautiful," her cousin Susan protested. For a physical education teacher, she was surprisingly interested in cathedrals, and never missed a church of any dimensions if she could help it.

"Oh, *churches!*" Barbara shrugged a tanned shoulder exposed by her thin halter. She wore shorts, too, which made her quite a problem when they wanted to go into a cathedral. The Mexicans got stony-faced or openly abusive if she went in like that. Not, thought Mrs. Wagstaff amusedly, that any of her other clothes would have changed matters much. Her dresses were all thin, cut to the waist or slashed strategically to show smooth strips of thigh or midriff. The clothes, though, were probably just a symptom. What they said, without perhaps her being aware of it herself, was that she needed attention . . . and she was beautifully constructed to get it. At Oaxaca, for instance, she had managed to get herself lost in the evening market and they had all had to wait in the bus more than an hour until José came back with her clinging to his arm. She had, she told them—with relish—run away from the attentions of a native far gone in tequila and gotten confused in the narrow, darkening streets. "It was *lovely* to see José," she said, her green eyes melting up into his face.

"We should all have spread out and looked," said Mr. Cartwright shortly. "We'd have found you in half the time!"

Barbara smiled, brushed her bare arm against his, and climbed demurely up the steps of the bus, leaving his dark, ruddy face with an expression that could only be called *molten*. Mrs. Wagstaff's odd, urchin grin curled the sides of her mouth. The pretty creature was so obvious. How extraordinary that men shouldn't notice how she played them on her line. Or perhaps they did . . . and liked it. More likely that . . . though men *could* be remarkably obtuse. She thought of a few turns she had played on Gerald before their marriage, and smiled again. He had had no idea of how determined she had been to be Mrs. Gerald Wagstaff. She gazed down at the broad shelf of her bosom and sighed a great gust through her Roman nose. Then, just to be sure, she held her breath and counted. Ever since she had been driven off a wharf into deep water, she had worked on her breathing. She'd been pulled right out, fortunately, but what if she hadn't? Pearl divers would have survived where she did not. So now, at odd moments, she worked on her breath control. She had it up to three minutes and forty seconds. Of course her practicing, coming as it did at any moment of stress, *did* occasionally startle people.

She still *did* get rather red in the face, but that was a small price to pay for her increasing confidence about being caught under water.

Outside the bus, flat, level fields of spiky plants went on endlessly. "Henequen," said José in answer to Mrs. Crummit's question. "It is to make fiber for the rope factory we saw in Mérida."

It was a tedious plant, just clusters of spiky swords, and it was the only thing to see for miles. Every now and then they passed a dusty little village of huts. Through the single door openings in front, they could see hammocks slung from the walls. A few chickens scratched in the dooryards and fluffed dust into their feathers.

"Ugh," said Barbara. "Why did anyone ever want to settle *here?*"

"We'll have to ask your father that," said Mrs. Gibson acidly.

Barbara looked at her coolly. "Well, I'm sure he'd *know!*" she said. She never talked of her father very personally, but she rarely let an opportunity go by to show off his eminence. And, indeed, Dr. Lawrence Canning *was* an eminent archaeologist. But where had he been while she was growing up, Mrs. Wagstaff wondered, to have had so little intellectual impact on her? In some clutter of ruins digging, no doubt. Where he *still* was, in fact. Only the fact that Dr. Canning was working at Chichén Itzá could account for her presence on this tour. She had insisted on going to visit him during her college inter-term. "He was awfully *busy,*" she said importantly, "but he was dying to see me too. So here I am!" It sounded rather as though the poor child needed to think so, Mrs. Wagstaff thought. It couldn't have been easy for a motherless child who looked like Barbara to have so busy a father!

He must have thought the bus trip would be educational for her. Certainly it couldn't have occurred to him that it would be educational for the rest of them! She looked around at her fellow tourists. Surely he could hardly have figured out a safer way for her to travel than with her field-hockey playing cousin Susan and a carload of elderly tourists.

"Well," Mrs. Crummit said, looking out at the dreary landscape, "why *did* they settle here?"

"The people were pushed down here by other civilizations more warlike," said José, his dark eyes still resting on Barbara.

"Yech," she said. "It's so *dull.* Not even a stream or a tiny hill!"

"Where people live is not dull to *them.*" José's voice was stiff. "It was a challenging environment, and it produced wonders, as you will see." José's English was almost too good. It smacked of the schoolroom and reminded them that he was himself from a village in Yucatán. Perhaps even descended from the Maya. Though his nose, Mrs. Wagstaff thought, was too good by far. Nobody would call the Maya a good-looking people!

"They'd never get *me* to live in a place like this, challenge or not," said Barbara brightly, her eyes on the tiresome, flat fields bouncing by outside the smoked blue windows. But then she smiled radiantly at José, and his fine, brown fingers relaxed on the arms of the chair he had facing them from the front of the bus.

They were all thoroughly tired and bored when they suddenly passed a great mountain upthrust at the sky on their left.

"Wait! Oh, what is it?" Susan almost thrust her dark head through the window. "Oh, *look!*"

"Yes," said José, his dark face lit with pride. "It is the temple of Kukulcan. Do you want to stop now, or shall we go first to the hacienda for a rest?"

"Oh, *now,*" breathed Susan.

"Yes, indeed," said Professor Michelson, his round, bearded face bright with enthusiasm.

"Oh, no," said Barbara wearily. "Let's go to the hotel and clean up. There'll be lots of time for the old ruins! Besides—" she looked around quickly—"Mrs. Cartwright needs a rest!"

Mrs. Cartwright, sunken like a vegetable in her wheelchair, made no motion or sound.

"Well," said José, "perhaps its *would* be best to go first to the hotel."

The driver began to pick up speed and the incredible mound of masonry retreated behind them. Susan gave a sharp little sigh of disappointment, but she said nothing. Mrs. Wagstaff guessed that Dr. Canning was paying her fare . . . and a companion didn't argue with the boss.

"You must be so anxious to see your father," said Mrs. Crummit kindly to Barbara.

"Yes," she said. "I haven't seen him since September. He's been so *busy!*" Her green gaze flickered out the window and then, seeing nothing of interest, settled dreamily on José's hands.

THE HOTEL WAS A CHARMING HACIENDA SET IN A tropical garden. On the white, arched terrace a peacock posed haughtily. Cottages were scattered among the flowering trees, and a swimming pool was a shimmer of turquoise in a bower of oleanders.

"This was a famous hacienda," said José, as his little troupe stood looking about. "There have been terrible massacres here and much blood."

"Enough to give any hotel a good name," said Mrs. Wagstaff. "Not to speak of the fact that John Lloyd Stephens stayed here in 1842."

"Well before the massacre, I believe," added Professor Michelson. The professor was a small sparrow of a man with a bright eye, a very bald head, and a curly foam of white beard that engulfed his ears. There was little he didn't know about the Celts in Britain, and he was reading up on the Maya much too fast for any guide's pleasure.

José looked at them both darkly. "Yes, that is so," he said shortly. "Would you all like to see your rooms now?"

They would. In a few minutes he and two Mayan bellboys in white pajamas had disposed them all in their various cottages and were bringing the mounds of luggage in from the bus. There was certainly nothing bloody to be seen in the sunny view from the cottage verandahs. Bees hummed peaceably in the mock orange and fuchsia flowers, and a couple of gardeners were trifling with emerald green grass with what looked like nail scissors.

Mrs. Wagstaff looked around in satisfaction. Probably the plumbing wouldn't work—it rarely did in Mexico—but the place was lovely: red-tiled floors, antique-looking chests, a bedside lamp (*most* necessary, and most rare), and fresh towels. There were even flowers in a bright blue glass vase. She took out *The Death of a Hittite*, put it down beside the bed, and gave a great, gusty snort of pleasure. She had bagged it from the hotel kiosk in Mérida just as Professor Michelson's hand came out to pluck it for himself. He had roared a little . . . but given in, and she had promised to pass it on as soon as she had finished. Now looking at it, she foresaw a pleasant evening tucked up with a literate murder. She and the professor were both fans, but unfortunately their tastes tended in different directions. The professor had a predilection for tough detectives who were always getting hit on the head because they never looked behind doors. She much preferred the kind of murder that was committed in the Cambridge University library by a don who left clues in classical Latin. It was unfortunate because it made their exchanges somewhat difficult, and the supply was small. Nevertheless, an addict will adapt to even a watered drug if nothing else is available. It seemed possible that *Death of a Hittite* might partly suit them both.

The rest of the day looked restful *and* stimulating. She went in to test the plumbing. But it wasn't the plumbing that was the problem. Almost at once Mrs. Wagstaff found the fly in all this ointment. The cottages were double, and from the other end of the wall voices came with total clarity.

"Brian!" A sound like the meeting of two bolsters, and then a silence, a gasp, and a high giggle. "Wait. I can't breathe!" But there was no respite. Instead, skirmishing noises, smacking sounds, the creak of a bedspring. Mrs. Wagstaff stood rigid in the middle of her bedroom and listened. There was not much choice . . . and in any case, she believed in listening. "If you are too old to act, you need *some* vicarious pleasures," she would have said if anyone had dared ask her.

The silence was brief. "Barb! Oh, *God,* I love you!" a man's rather high voice whispered, it almost seemed, in Mrs. Wagstaff's ear.

"But where's *Daddy?*" Barbara's voice was breathless, but taut. "After I come all the way to this frightful place, why isn't he here to meet me?"

"Oh, he'll be back soon. Barbara, marry me right away. *Now!* I want you so much I . . ."

"Brian, wait. Now *wait!*"

"Where's your ring? You're not wearing it!"

"I am too. It's just that . . . look, I've got it here, on this chain."

"On a chain? Why not on your finger?" He sounded accusing.

"It's too big. I have to get it fixed. But Brian . . . where *is* Daddy?"

The man seemed to come back to that subject with effort. "He had to go to Mexico City. He said to tell you he'll be back tomorrow. He sent his love and said he was very sorry, but he won't be long."

"Oh, damn! I don't see why he had to go just *now!*" Her voice had the note of a child disappointed in an adult once *again.*

"It was a dig problem, and it couldn't wait. He's left me in charge. Never mind, Barbara. Barbara? . . ." There was a scuffling sound, and then silence.

In the stillness the sound of sandals slapping on the verandah tiles was sharp. The door next door opened briskly, and a horrified voice said "Oh! Sorry!"

"You might knock! Well, never mind. It's just Susan, Brian. Susan, do you remember Brian Bothwell? Daddy's assistant?" Barbara's voice sounded complacent.

"Yes. Yes, of course. Glad to see you again." Susan sounded hoarse as though she had just caught a cold and would have liked to be in bed in Timbuktu.

"How are you, Susan. Good trip?" The words were polite, but the tone was uncomfortable.

"Lovely. It's fascinating country."

"Ugh," said Barbara.

"Great traveler, Barbara, isn't she?" The rather reedy man's voice was suddenly full of indulgent possessiveness.

"Well," said Susan stiffly, "I'll just have a look around before lunch. See you later."

The door opened and closed once more, and the slap of sandals was suddenly silenced on the garden path. Mrs. Wagstaff sighed and eased her corset with a faint creak. A walk seemed a good idea. She did not, after all, want the frustration of listening to *all* of Barbara's love life.

She closed her own door and turned the key. It was not wise to make temptation too tempting. She moved off down the earthen path toward the main house, but she had gone only as far as the blue swimming pool when she heard a curious, hammering sound coming from . . . a tree? She swung her large bosom toward the tree and listened. The sound came again . . . a muffled woodpecker? Mrs. Wagstaff was not a birdwatcher, but she had a large curiousity and a firm nature. Briskly she marched toward the vine-hung tree and looked behind it.

Susan stood there banging her fist against the trunk. She turned a flushed, furious face toward Mrs. Wagstaff, and pulled her hand down. "Oh, damn!" she said. With her usual reserve utterly dissolved, she looked young and vulnerable. She was a tall, big-boned girl, but her eyes were an attractive dark blue, and her hair, although she wore it pulled hard back into a ponytail with a rubber band, was a glossy black. She isn't really all that plain, Mrs. Wagstaff decided. It was just the contrast with the ravishing Barbara that made her seem so.

It was the contrast that was the trouble, obviously.

"Tell me what the problem is," Mrs. Wagstaff commanded. "You'll feel better. Is it that young man?"

The girl's dark eyes flew up, startled. "How do you . . . oh, what difference does it make?" She shook her head as if to dash away cobwebs, and stood up very straight. "Some people always get everything, don't they?" she said, a grim, desolate note in her voice.

"It certainly seems that way sometimes. But you can't always tell. Remember, "Richard Cory, one calm summer night, /Went home and put a bullet through his head"!

Susan suddenly laughed. "Thanks," she said. "I'd forgotten Richard Cory. I'm sorry to be such a fool. It's just that . . . well, actually, I met him first! At Uncle Larry's office. And he's not at all Barbara's type. He's a real scholar . . . like her father."

Mrs. Wagstaff looked at the girl thoughtfully. "Perhaps that's why she's in love with him."

"But she *isn't*. Not really. She's just sort of got him all . . . tied up. He doesn't even remember meeting me! That's the kind of impact *I* make!"

Mrs. Wagstaff considered the girl before her. "It doesn't need to be," she said decidedly. "You play up that dreary idea of yourself, that's your problem. Why else would you pull your pretty hair back so hard and wear that horrid pale lipstick? Let your hair down. Redden your mouth. Compete! Why not! What have you got to lose that you haven't lost already?"

The girl stared at her. "Compete?"

"Certainly. You're a great deal prettier than I ever was, but I got the man *I* wanted. Take chances. Throw your hat in the ring. We pass this way only once, you know."

It was good advice, but it would come back to haunt Mrs. Wagstaff later. She was always sticking her two cents in, trying to manage everyone. Not a good idea, Gerald had always said. It was just that she *saw*, so much more clearly than people themselves, how to make their living better and happier. And of course it was uncharitable not to *show* them!

LUNCH WAS IN A COOL, HIGH-CEILINGED ROOM
overlooking the gardens. The tour group . . . four tables' worth . . .
was waited on by tiny, plump, brown girls in embroidered huipils
. . . a kind of long, white mumu. Susan, sitting with Barbara, the
Cartwrights, and a strange young man, was wearing her black hair
down on her shoulders. When Mrs. Wagstaff nodded at her approvingly from the next table, she frowned, turned scarlet, and bent to
pick up her dropped napkin.

Well, thought Mrs. Wagstaff, she still isn't wearing any makeup,
but it's a first step. She looked consideringly at the young man to
see what the fuss was about. Barbara had mentioned at least once
a day how brilliant her father's assistant was, but if he *was*, it wasn't
the sort of brilliance one would expect Barbara to respond to. He
was tall, not very muscular, though those sinewy men could be
deceptive that way. His face was utterly forgettable, except for light
blue eyes enormously enlarged by thick, horn-rimmed glasses. An
academic type, Mrs. Wagstaff would have said . . . and she *knew*
academic types . . . but not the sort to send female blood racing.

There was no way to tell what was happening to Barbara's blood, but Bothwell's seemed to be nicely on the boil. His odd eyes, which were his most interesting feature, were riveted on Barbara, and barely left her face long enough for him to eat. Barbara was being enchantingly gay, comparing her golden-tan arm first with Bothwell's rope-veined brown one and then with Mr. Cartwright's hairy, muscular one. Susan was silent, fiercely engaged with her soup.

"May I introduce our guide?" José Bunuelos stood beside the table with a short, dark-faced man who could have climbed down off a Mayan frieze. For all his short stature, he looked powerful. His nose was the great, bowed hook of all the ancient carvings. It made Mrs. Wagstaff finger her own redoubtable nose and wonder briefly if she, too, was descended from a frieze.

"How do you do," she said. "Are you the expert on these ruins? It will be helpful to have a specialist along on our expedition." She nodded like a duchess.

José's handsome brown face stiffened. Perhaps he considered that *he* was a sufficient specialist ... but he gave no other sign. " He knows everything about Chichén," he said gravely. "Luis Ruz."

The new man inclined his head the smallest possible amount. He did not smile. Mrs. Crummit fluttered nervously at him. Mrs. Gibson looked severe. Apparently nothing tempted Señor Ruz to speech. His brown, immobile face simply turned away as the two men moved off to the next table.

Barbara looked at Mr. Ruz with the eye of a woman for whom all men were potentially interesting.

"But I thought *you* were our guide, José," she said.

"I believe," said Mr. Cartwright, "that Mr. Ruz has been assigned to us especially to do Chichén Itzá."

"Oh. Well, that's fine," said Barbara. "After all, the more the merrier!" She smiled radiantly at Mr. Ruz and reached out her hand. There was an odd moment of silence. Mr. Cartwright's dark, rather saturnine face seemed patched with red. José's dark eyes fastened themselves intently on the golden glow of Barbara's bare shoulders. For a second it looked as though her outstretched hand would be ignored. Then Mr. Ruz slowly raised his hand, took hers, and squeezed. She gave a tiny yelp, and pulled away.

"Wow," she said. "What a grip!" But her glance was more interested than ever.

"Well, if you're finished," said Bothwell in a hard voice, ignoring the guides, "perhaps you should all get started."

"Aren't *you* coming, Brian?" She seized his arm.

"Not much point, is there? You'll have lots of company. And I know these ruins backwards. Your father's left me in charge, so I've got to get back to work. I'll see you for cocktails around five." He rose as the guides moved away, and looked down at Barbara's blonde head. She was calmly taking a last sip of coffee, as everyone else got hurriedly to his feet. Only Mrs. Wagstaff, who never allowed herself to be hurried, was still sitting, and heard Bothwell's last remark. Susan's arm, her *tennis* arm, Mrs. Wagstaff thought, grew hard as though she were wielding a racket, but she said nothing.

"Don't get too friendly with the guides, Barbara. They may not understand."

"Understand what?" Her cheeks dimpled mischievously. "Oh, Brian, don't be *silly!*"

They started with La Iglesia, a strange little building magnificently carved all over with snakes, heads, and strange, coiling designs.

"Where did they hold services?" asked Mrs. Crummit blankly, looking about the bare interior.

"Not a church like *your* church," Mr. Ruz said, an edge of contempt in his heavily accented words.

"Then why do they call it that?" demanded Mrs. Gibson, determined to get her money's worth of information.

José, who seemed rather tense this afternoon, gave Mr. Ruz a forbidding look and interrupted. "It was a name given by the archaeologists later. Many buildings were named so."

"Yes," said Mrs. Wagstaff helpfully. "Casa de las Monjas had nothing to do with nuns, I am sure . . . nor the temple of the warriors with warriors, I dare say."

Mr. Ruz's expression was almost malevolent. "You have no use for guide," he said, his black eyes sharp on Mrs. Wagstaff's face.

"Oh, but I do indeed. I've read all the books, of course, but that's not the same thing as being on the spot, is it?" Mrs. Wagstaff was unruffled. "Where do we go next?"

"Casa de las Monjas," said Mr. Ruz shortly.

The group trailed after him to an even more richly ornamented building a short distance away.

"Oh, look," cried Susan, "Elephant trunks. How would they know about elephants *here*?" She pointed upward to where a series of what did look like elephant trunks projected down the corners of the building.

"Are noses of the God, not elephant," said Mr. Ruz.

Susan tripped along after him as they circled the building staring at the hieroglyphs, the carved masks, the snake designs. Mr. Ruz made a peculiar guide, Mrs. Wagstaff thought. He seemed to answer all Susan's questions in monosyllables . . . and he paid very little attention to the further education of the group.

As if to make up for Mr. Ruz, José talked with great speed, rattling off, like a memorized book, all the details Mrs. Wagstaff knew just as well herself. When they crossed the hot, bare field toward the great circular building called the Caracol, it was José's raised voice they all heard:

"The Caracol was an astronomical observatory. The only other such circular building is at Mayapan. This one, you see, sits on top of a great stone platform. The doorways open toward the four points of the compass. Very exactly. The temple . . ."

"Do we have to go up all those steps?" demanded Mrs. Gibson. "My heavens, those people must have had great leg muscles!"

"It is very interesting inside," said José. "There is a circular staircase . . ."

"I had enough circular staircases at St. Peter's last year," said Mrs. Gibson. "I'll wait for you right here!"

"In that case," said Mrs. Wagstaff, "you can stay with Mrs. Cart-

wright while her husband goes up." There was no question in her
voice.

"Oh, no . . . that's not necessary . . . I . . ." began Mr. Cartwright.

"Oh, go on," said Mrs. Gibson ungraciously. "Go right ahead.
Only don't be too long." She turned her hot, red face toward Mrs.
Cartwright and said, as if the invalid were a child, "I'll be right here
now, so don't worry." Mrs. Cartwright couldn't speak, but her large,
gray eyes contracted slightly, and the fingers of her left hand
twitched on the arms of her chair.

Mrs. Wagstaff was turning away when something—an odd immobility in his posture—made her look at Mr. Cartwright. He was
looking at his wife like a man in pain, his mouth contorted in anguish. It was only a moment. Then he gave her a quick pressure on
the shoulder and started up the steps fast. When Mrs. Wagstaff
caught up with him, he was standing with Barbara and José near the
top. José was talking rapidly of the miracles of Mayan astronomy.
"One door points to the south; one points to the place where the
moon sets farthest south in the year; one points . . ."

"What did they want to know all that *for*?" asked Barbara wearily,
pushing a blonde tendril back from her damp forehead. "What
good did it do them?"

Mr. Ruz's hooded black eyes flashed in the dimness of the passage. "Was necessary for harvest," he said. "To know the gods and
all their ways."

"Much good it did them!" She shrugged a bare shoulder. "Where
are they *now*?" There wasn't much point to people who couldn't
even survive, she implied. Mr. Ruz didn't answer. He walked on
ahead up the curving stone steps. It was Mrs. Wagstaff who seized
the ball.

"Nobody knows what happened to them," she said. "They don't
know whether famine came, or plague, whether the water dried up
or the people revolted against their priests and left. It is one of the
great mysteries."

"Well, it's a bore, *I* think. What's the point of harping on all these
dead things?"

"You only live once?" inquired Mrs. Wagstaff. Barbara's full, pink lips opened.

"Yes, that's exactly what I was going to say!"

"Yes," said Mr. Cartwright in a strange, hoarse voice. "The big thing is living *now*, isn't it?" And suddenly, as if the impulse was uncontrollable, he reached out and took Barbara's golden arm in his hand. José's face darkened. Barbara looked down at the hand and then up, with a bright, hard smile, into Mr. Cartwright's face.

"You *do* agree with me, don't you?" she said. "You can't imagine how bored I am with this endless business of digging things up. Like my father. He's only interested in things after they're a thousand years old and in a museum case!" Her voice was full of an old resentment. Then she looked again at Mr. Cartwright's hand and malice flashed in her green eyes. "I wish I'd had someone like *you* . . . for a father!" she said.

Mr. Cartwright flushed a deep, brick red, and his hand dropped from Barbara's arm.

"I guess we go that way," he said harshly, and strode ahead through the passage. José followed.

"That was a little hard on the male ego," Mrs. Wagstaff said mildly.

"Well, he deserved it. Really!"

"Poor man. He can't be more than forty-five. It must be hard with his wife so stricken."

She shrugged her dainty shoulders. "Well, I can't help *that*, can I? He's always hanging around and trying to touch me. Ugh!" And she ran lightly on up the curving stairs.

MRS. WAGSTAFF WAS TAKING HER EVENING WALK. SHE
had taken an evening walk every day for forty years. It had become
a ritual like brushing her great mound of tan hair fifty times and her
teeth seventy-five. For years Gerald had gone with her, to "protect"
her. But for eight years now, she had gone alone. She had walked
along the river in Verona, beside Bangkok canals, through the night
streets of Tokyo, under the palm trees of Samoa—all sorts of places
where women are not supposed to go alone. But no one had tried
grabbing her for the white slave trade, no one had even pinched her.
It was quite frustrating, she often thought. But the habit was too
ingrained to stop, even though it was a bit late in the day for amor-
ous adventure. She walked through the gardens like a major general, her head upright, the scented air whistling gently through her
eagle nose. She held her breath once and achieved three minutes
and fifty seconds. A small triumph. When she got up to four
minutes, she would take up scuba diving. It would be good to know
that if anything went wrong with that bulky equipment, she would
have four minutes in which to rise.

The moon was up, but the garden, basking in the cool radiance, was empty. The tour group, exhausted from its day of climbing steps in the hot sun was, she thought, disposed in its cottages, collapsed on the beds, washing out nylon underwear or reading Agatha Christie mysteries. Mrs. Wagstaff had read all of Agatha Christie, but she thought pleasantly of the new mystery beside her bed, waiting for her. For the moment, she was enjoying the peaceful garden. Although Mrs. Wagstaff was glad to do her bit in telling people how to get the most out of life, sometimes they seemed to her too silly to bother about. In moments like this, she preferred solitude and deep breathing.

But solitude was always the hardest commodity in the world to come by. For the garden was not empty after all. She rounded a curve in the path and heard a great, plunging splash from the swimming pool ahead. And laughter. Girlish, provocative laughter.

"Come back!" And another splash. The moonlight on the pool was cut into jagged ribbons, and two bodies rose together and merged, dark hands holding a pale, moonlight-colored head.

Mrs. Wagstaff stood in the shadow of the oleander bush and surveyed the scene. Clearly Barbara was not one of those who wasted her time on laundry or on mysteries. Treading water, she arched herself backward, put both arms around José's head and pulled him down under the water, her mouth not leaving his. They disappeared under the milky surface. Mrs. Wagstaff waited, she guessed two minutes and a half—not bad for amateurs—but they rose at last, Barbara gasping . . . and angry.

"Who do you think you are?" she demanded, coughing, her hands pushing against his dark chest. "You . . . you *native!* Get away from me!" She arced her legs like a spring and sliced sideways through the water away from him.

"Bar-ba-ra! Wait. What have I done? Bar-ba-ra!"

But Bar-ba-ra was already at the other side of the pool, climbing out, pulling up the bottoms of her bikini, which were halfway down her golden thighs. José had clearly found her invitation too much for his control. Just as clearly, he didn't understand her anger. After all, had she not kissed him? Had she not seemed to want him? Mrs.

Wagstaff's broad mouth stretched sardonically. Poor fellow. All his good English and his experience with elderly tourists didn't help him much in understanding the outrage of an American teaser who expected to call all the turns herself.

"Bar-ba-ra. Please to wait! I am coming!"

But Barbara was not pleased to wait. Before he could get to the side of the pool the girl's bare feet were pounding down the path. She passed within inches of Mrs. Wagstaff, her lovely face wet and scowling. She was not wearing Bothwell's ring around her neck.

In another moment José stood at the edge of the pool, his brown, lithe figure tensed to pursue. Then a door slammed. He clenched his fists, stared into the darkness a moment, and then sat down heavily on the coping of the pool. Mrs. Wagstaff, about to tiptoe away, had her head turned toward the path when she heard a voice behind her.

"Fool!" The voice rasped like a snake striking. Mrs. Wagstaff started, and turned to defend herself. But there was no need. The description—though she would not have debated it at the moment —was not for her. Luis Ruz, the ruins guide, was staring down at José, his face a mask of outrage.

"Don't you know you are only a *native!* You fool!"

José's face rose fiercely. "I am not. I am . . ."

"I *know* who you are. You are worse than a native. They know their places. But *you* . . ."

José got to his feet in one swift, catlike movement. "Be still!" he said. "I will not be talked to as a child. Leave me alone!" His face twisted with fury, he disappeared suddenly down another path, leaving Ruz staring after him.

Mrs. Wagstaff let her breath out carefully, but her corsets creaked, and Ruz's head whipped about in her direction. She stamped her feet in place, increasing the sound like someone walking toward the pool. It was a childhood trick. Then brushing the bushes aside with loud carelessness, she stepped onto the moonlit verge of the pool.

"Ah, Señor Ruz," she said grandly, her great pile of hair nodding at him. "It is a beautiful evening, is it not?"

But it was evidently no time for pleasantry. The dark face looked

at her a moment as though she were some strange, reptilian creature, and then Mr. Ruz had gone, leaving her alone at last to con-
template the silent garden.

"BUT HOW COULD THEY GET A BALL INTO THAT LITTLE hole?" Mrs. Gibson demanded, staring up. "That's impossible!"

They were in the long ball court of the Maya. A strange place where, José explained, the Maya used to play an even stranger game. Two brick walls made a broad alley on the sun-hardened earth, half the length of a football field. About nine feet up on each wall a stone ring projected from the brick into the alley. Into this, as into a basketball net, the Mayan ball was to be sent. But it was far harder than basketball, for the ball could not be touched with the hands, and the ring, set at right angles to the wall, was an almost impossible angle for the players to aim at with their heads, hips, or knees.

"It *is* hard," José said. "But the game was a religious ritual. They played until someone got the ball through the ring." José was paying a great deal of attention to his charges . . . all but Barbara. He had given her a look of flame when she first appeared, but he had said nothing.

"Well, isn't that nice," said Mrs. Crummit. "I think it's lovely that even games should have a religious side. All *our* players ever do is sing the 'Star Spangled Banner.' "

"I'm not sure you would have cared for this particular religious side," said Mrs. Wagstaff. She turned, smiling, to Mr. Ruz.

He looked at her silently from a face like wet bronze.

Since it was clear that he was not going to explain, and Crummit was waiting with birdlike interest, Mrs. Wagstaff went on.

"There are two teams, each with a captain. They keep playing until one side scores." She paused impressively. They were all listening now. "Then the winning captain takes the losing captain and —cuts off his head!"

Mrs. Crummit stared at her, her moist, pink face growing pale. "What?"

"Yes indeed," said Mrs. Wagstaff with scholarly relish. "He cuts off his opponent's head. It's part of a ritual, where the blood is an offering to the god. Blood was an important offering. They used to cut their earlobes and penises too."

The silence was absolute.

"I don't believe it!" said Mrs. Gibson at last. Mrs. Crummit was speechless. She had never heard anyone use *that* word before.

"Quite true!" said Professor Michelson firmly, his round, brown eyes cast piously upward. "Religion is a wonderful thing."

José looked angry, as if his relatives were being impugned. "The head *was* cut off," he said. "It was a rite. The players were not forced, however. They *chose* to play!" He gestured at the wall beside them. "The ceremony is there, on the stone."

They clustered to look.

In low relief on the bricks there was indeed an Indian kneeling and another holding a machete in one hand and a head in the other. The head must have been cut off only moments before, since the body to which it belonged had not yet even fallen over.

"Yech!" said Barbara, her delicate nose wrinkled in disgust.

Mrs. Cartwright's head bobbled on her thin neck, but her gray eyes were riveted to the wall. Mrs. Crummit looked dazed, and a tiny whimper of sound came from her throat. The sun struck down at them like a hammer.

"Autres temps, autres mores," said the professor, his eyes bright with interest. He turned to speak to José, but Jose and Mr. Ruz had turned away and were leading the group out of the ball court.

It did Mrs. Crummit no good at all that the next sight was a giant stone phallus looming into the air a good five feet over her head. She had consented to have her picture taken beside it before anyone mentioned what it was.

"Say," said Harrison Gumbiner, who sold trusses and prosthetic devices back home in Kansas, "is this thing what I think it is?"

Mrs. Crummit, her arm about the stone, smiling brightly into Barbara's camera, glanced sideways at him without moving. She *did* want a good picture for her daughter.

"Well, I know what it looks like," said Mrs. Gibson grimly, "and I wouldn't send a picture of it to *my* daughter!"

Mrs. Crummit's eyes fluttered up the shaft beside her, bewildered.

"It's a . . . phallic symbol, isn't it?" asked Mrs. Bernardi.

"That's no symbol," Mr. Gumbiner grinned, wiping his bald head. "That's the real thing!"

"Oh!" Mrs. Crummit, still staring upward, suddenly dropped her arm from the stone as if it were burned. "Oh . . . oh . . ." she said, backing away, her face scarlet.

"You *moved*," Barbara laughed.

Mrs. Wagstaff put her arm around Mrs. Crummit, who was looking faint. "I think it's time we got in out of the sun," she boomed, and swept Mrs. Crummit around and toward the bus.

At lunch Brian Bothwell appeared, looking hot and dusty. He was there, he said, just to tell Barbara that her father had phoned and wouldn't make it back until the next morning. She was to stay with the party till then.

"Oh, *no*," she said, looking around at the tour company. It was not a complimentary glance." Why can't I go to the dig and stay there instead of hanging around with these . . ." The last word wasn't quite audible. It might, Mrs. Wagstaff thought, have been "creeps" or "cretins" . . . something with a *cr*.

Bothwell's big hand tightened on her bare shoulder. "I'm just telling you what he said. The dig house is a mess, Barbara. You're better off . . ."

"Yech!" Her perfect little nose twitched. The dining room was as silent as though the twenty-two people in it had just gone mute.

Nevertheless, to Mrs. Wagstaff's surprise, Barbara came along on the afternoon trip to the great pyramid. She wanted a picture to take back to school, she said to Mr. Cartwright. And somehow he found himself carrying her camera as well as his own. He walked beside her with both cameras slung over his shoulder, pushing his wife's chair.

"What technique!" Mrs. Wagstaff thought, with the admiration of one manipulator for another. Give her an important enough lever and a girl like that could rule the world. Suppose, instead of Mr. Cartwright, the president of the United States . . . or Mr. Brezhnev . . . or Mao Tse-tung . . . were on her leash? A snort of amusement whistled through her nose.

The picture Barbara wanted was a standard tourist shot, but with her as its center, it looked somehow original, even exciting. The great pyramid of Kukulcan loomed up in the middle of a sunbaked field. Narrow steps ran up two sides of it all the way to a little stone temple at the top, the house of the sacrifices. There must have been two hundred steps, none more than about five inches wide, and there was nothing to hold onto but a rope of twisted metal that was fastened at the top and bottom.

Barbara ran lightly up the first ten or twelve steps without touching the rope. But then she glanced over her shoulder, stared for a moment at the steepness below her, and reached quickly for the handhold. "Wow!" she said. Professor Michelson, climbing behind her, was gallant. "I'll catch you," he said, "don't worry!"

She looked down at him. "I'd like a picture alone . . . if you don't mind," she said.

"No, no. Certainly not. Just a moment." He sidled clumsily sideways, his curly beard almost brushing the stone, getting out of the line of the camera. With nothing to hold onto, he suddenly froze, half lying against the steps.

"There. Take it now!" Barbara had gone up another twenty steps or so and her golden face glanced provocatively over her shoulder as she stretched her legs to look as though she were making a supreme, Everest-climbing effort. Spread-eagled against that incredible flight of steps, she looked the perfect heroine . . . Pauline in peril.

"Have you got it?"

Mr. Cartwright's dark head was bent over the finder. He clicked the shutter. At once, without another upward glance, she backed down the steps as agilely as a monkey, hand over hand along the metal rope.

"Anyone else want to climb up?" asked José.

The ladies rustled and smiled, shaking their heads.

"Professor Michelson," called Mrs. Wagstaff suddenly. There was no answer. With the precipitation of a charging buffalo, she began to climb the pyramid, her great, square bulk moving with astonishing speed. When she got to the step the professor was on, she moved sideways, holding onto the rope and stretching out her other arm.

"Take hold," she commanded loudly, "It's all right now."

He lifted his face from the stone and looked at her. "Damn it," he said. "I can't!"

"Certainly you can," she said. "Take my hand. I've got a good grip on the rope." She reached until her fingertips touched his shirt and suddenly, with a convulsive jerk, he shot out his arm and grasped her hand.

"Good. Now just slide along toward me."

He obeyed her absolutely, sliding along the step until he could grasp her dress. She backed down a couple of steps, detached his hand from hers, and reattached it to the metal rope. José had come up, but by then it was all over. Professor Michelson, his only hairless stretch of skin—his head—white and dripping with sweat, teetered down to the ground.

"You saved my life!" he said hoarsely, when he had reached the bottom. "I couldn't move."

"I know," she said. "It's vertigo. A lot of people have it."

"You were marvelous," Mrs. Crummit said, pink with admiration.

"Not at all," said Mrs. Wagstaff calmly. "I've done a lot of mountain climbing. I have a head for heights, that's all."

"Well," said Mrs. Gibson, "I guess I'll do my climbing behind *you* from now on. If *any!* I still don't see why the steps had to be so narrow!"

"It was to make the symbol of a serpent climbing up. Processions wound back and forth like a snake. Isn't that it?" Mrs. Wagstaff looked at José for confirmation, but José was busy. He was talking quickly to Barbara, his brown hands gesticulating, his face grim. She stood half turned away from him, but there was a faint, Mona Lisa smile on her face . . . the smile of one who has heard it all before. Nor did she hear him out.

"I'm going back to the hotel," she said suddenly. "It's too hot!" And without a backward glance, she started off toward the road. Everyone looked after her in surprise. Susan made as if to follow, and then stopped with an odd little grimace of irritation. José's face was so stiff that he looked all at once as masklike as Mr. Ruz. "We go now to the Virgin's Pool," he said, and turned away without further comment. The air around him seemed vibrant with some emotion . . . anger . . . passion . . . hatred?

They trailed after him without enthusiasm. It *was* hot. The worst thing about guides, Mrs. Wagstaff remarked to the professor, was that they always felt that they had to give you your money's worth of sightseeing . . . and almost nobody ever wanted that much.

"Yes," said Professor Michelson. His color had come back and his curly beard jutted forward rakishly once more. "Well, if we have to see more today, I will opt for the Virgin's Pool."

"What's that?" asked Mr. Gumbiner. "Anything like a typists' pool?" He grinned.

"It's where they used to sacrifice young girls by throwing them into a kind of well."

"Hey! *Alive?*"

"I believe so, though we don't know all the details." Mrs. Wagstaff was regretful. She disliked not knowing details.

"It sure takes all kinds, doesn't it?" said Mr. Gumbiner, shaking his freckled head." I suppose everybody has to get his kicks *somehow!*"

They had left the field and were walking down a grassy road cut out of the forest. The afternoon was hot and nobody seemed to have much left to say. Then suddenly, the road ended, and they stood in a startled clump before a sight none of them had quite expected. Brown, shaggy grass led to the edge of a fantastic pond. It was a tarn, really, with gray limestone walls rising straight up and enclosing, far below, a black, motionless bowl of water. There was no sound in the forest, and the water lay there without glint or reflection, a secretive, concealing presence. Even the birds were silent.

"What . . . is it?" Mrs. Crummit whispered at last. Mrs. Wagstaff, turning to answer, saw, or fancied she saw, an odd sight. Mr. Cartwright's large, red hands had opened and hung over the handles of his wife's wheelchair, not touching them. The chair, on a slight slope, stirred a trifle. Mrs. Cartwright's gray eyes stared upward in what looked like terror. The weird, loonlike cry came from her mouth, jarring them all. It was all over in a second. The red hands clenched firmly on the handles, and the cry bubbled away into silence.

"Boy," said Mr. Gumbiner softly, near Mrs. Wagstaff's ear. "How's that for sound effects?" He seemed to have noticed nothing else. Mrs. Wagstaff drew a deep breath and held it. She had forgotten her watch, but she found it calming anyway.

"What *is* down there?" asked Mrs. Gibson crossly. "It's an ugly thing, I *must* say."

"Sacrifices to the gods made here," José said. "Copal, gold jewelry . . .

"Virgins," Mr. Cartwright interrupted harshly.

José's face twitched. He seemed not to enjoy references to the bloodthirsty Mayan rites. "Yes," he said. "For the Gods, all things must be offered. All things worthy."

"Edward Thompson dredged this place," Mrs. Wagstaff said contemplatively.

"What did he find?" Mrs. Crummit asked.

Mrs. Wagstaff smiled. "As José says, copal, gold jewelry . . . and bones."

COCKTAILS WERE A GREAT SUCCESS. PROFESSOR
Michelson, having decided that Mrs. Wagstaff was his Joan of Arc,
seemed determined to pour indefinite quantities of tequila into her.
Since his upturning beard and caterpillar eyebrows had a goatlike
look, the tableau was rather like a painting of a satyr sporting about
Brunhilde.

"It may be," he said, "that we have our trip backwards. We should
perhaps spend two tenths of our time at the ruins . . . and eight
tenths here." And he refilled Mrs. Wagstaff's glass from the pitcher
of margaritas on the table.

Mrs. Wagstaff accepted her fourth margarita benignly. She had,
as Gerald had always said, a remarkable capacity. "A cast-iron stomach," was what he had said, precisely, though she thought it an
inelegant way to allude to her physical prowess.

Mr. Gumbiner was trying to get Mrs. Crummit to abandon sherry
for Scotch.

"Oh, I couldn't!" Mrs. Crummit gasped happily. "I can't think
what my daughter would say!"

"*I* can," said Barbara, and winked one green eye at Brian, who sat beside her. When she raised her empty martini glass for a refill, Brian, the stocky young bartender, and Mr. Cartwright almost lunged to take it. The bartender won, and went off with a ravening backward glance.

"Don't you think they have marvelous faces?" said Barbara, watching him. "So . . . I don't know . . . strong. You can just imagine them at all those bloody rituals." She looked down at her hand on the table, which was covered by Bothwell's fingers. "Like that Ruz man," she went on dreamily. "I bet he'd be . . . interesting."

"Barbara!" Bothwell's voice was hard. She glanced up sideways at him, withdrawing her hand as if un-noticing, and smiled radiantly into his face. His scowl did not change.

"Oh, Brian, don't be so silly!" She got up, took Mr. Cartwright's arm, and moved away with him. Her honey-colored hair shone like a Clairol ad, and her tight, white dress somehow took the color right out of Susan's red and gold print. It had done Susan no good, even with her pretty hair down, to go up to the dig that afternoon, Mrs. Wagstaff thought.

"Harvey," she said—and then paused just the right length of time—"May I call you Harvey? It's been such a long trip I feel we're old friends!"

"Yes, of course. Please *do.*" Cartwright's dark red face looked startled, but delighted. He was alone tonight, his wife apparently early off to bed.

"Tell me, Harvey," she went on, as they stood at the bar together, "what do you do? I've been trying to imagine." Her small, tanned hand rested trustingly on his arm.

"Do?" The image of Barbara wondering about him seemed, for a moment, to take away his powers of response. "Why, I'm just a businessman. I run an electronics firm in Rochester."

Mrs. Wagstaff, fascinated as always by Barbara's maneuvers, knew nothing of Mr. Cartwright's impoverished youth or his awkwardness with women, but she could see by his expression that Barbara had demolished him. The sight made her uncomfortable. She thought of Mrs. Cartwright crouched in her chair. How monstrously unfair life was! And there, across the room was another ... Susan, with lipstick on, chattering bravely to a Brian Bothwell whose light blue eyes roamed over her head to follow Barbara. Susan's eyes were on a level with Brian's. She was a tall girl. But she had not yet learned what to do with her body. *Socially,* that is. She must, Mrs. Wagstaff thought, have been great on a hockey field or a tennis court where she had something to *do.* Here, where her arms just hung empty, she looked awkward. If she had only had a rope to climb!

Thank God she was out of all that, thought Mrs. Wagstaff. It was so peaceful not to have to magnetize a man! Men were all very well, but far too much attention was always paid to them. They were spoiled, all of them, by the feverish desire of women to throw themselves under their chariot wheels. All, that is, except Barbara. As a liberated woman, Mrs. Wagstaff should have been on Barbara's team, perhaps, but Barbara wasn't really a liberated type. She was a siren, one of the Lorelei, whose goal was not equality but destruction. Still, it was interesting ... far more interesting than life in Minneapolis.

"That girl," said Professor Michelson, "reminds me of a student I had once. She had my whole class in a fever, and at the end of the year one of the boys killed himself over her. Jumped off a bridge."

"I think," said Mrs. Wagstaff consideringly, "that was a mistake. He should have smacked her and dragged her off to his lair." Her eyes followed Barbara. "There are some women for whom gentleness is precisely the wrong tactic."

The dinner gong ran.

If cocktails were a success, dinner was not. Everyone had drunk too much. Susan, finding herself placed beside Mrs. Bernardi, tried politely to talk, but soon retreated into silence. Barbara, radiating gin and sex appeal, chose to sit between Mr. Gumbiner and the professor. Bothwell, after a furious, pale glare at her, left the dining room. Mr. Cartwright, cast into outer darkness, was forced to sit at the next table with Mrs. Wagstaff and several of the blue-haired ladies.

"Tell me, Mr. Cartwright," Mrs. Wagstaff said, pushing her enchiladas aside, "has your wife been ill long?"

"What?" He fumbled at his water glass. "Oh. Yes. Well, it's about three years now." He looked as if the question had caught him beneath the sternum. But Mrs. Wagstaff had long ago decided that the way to find things out was to ask.

"It must be a great trouble," she said. "Does she understand what we say to her? It's hard to know in stroke cases, isn't it?"

"Yes. She understands everything . . . I think. She just can't talk. The nerves that control . . ." His voice trailed off.

"Yes, I see. I do hope the trip isn't tiring her too much."

"No. Of course not. Why should it? She has only to sit!" His voice was so bitter that Mrs. Wagstaff turned to her dinner. Gerald would have said she was being too nosy again. Sometimes it seemed to her a pity that she was so curious about everything. It did get her into so many uncomfortable situations. At other times, though, curiosity seemed the most important element in life. Without it, she would have died of boredom.

"It's a beautiful evening, isn't it?" she said neutrally, after a long, chewing pause. They were facing the terrace windows.

Mr. Cartwright stared out at the moonlit bougainvillea flowers. With a sudden, awkward lurch, he pushed away from the table and got up. "I'm not hungry," he said. Walking with a stiff dignity, he went out the terrace door, his eyes avoiding everyone, his napkin still clutched in his fingers.

"Well," said Mrs. Gibson, "*He's* got some manners. I suppose he couldn't stand women his own age!"

"Oh, he can't be *that* old," said Mrs. Crummit.

"Oh?" Mrs. Gibson flushed indignantly. "I don't know about *you*, but *I'm* not *that* old."

"I'm sorry. Oh, dear, I didn't mean you were. I just meant . . ."

"Well, we're none of us nymphs," said Mrs. Wagstaff. "Thank God." She put down her napkin. "It's time for my walk."

"If you think you can carry all those margaritas around," snapped Mrs. Gibson.

Mrs. Wagstaff smiled blandly. "They're not heavy. I'll manage."

It *was* a perfect evening. The air smelled like a wedding. Mrs. Wagstaff wandered far down the road until she could see the bulk of Kukulcan reared against the sky. She was about to turn into the field when a darker figure emerged from the shadow of the pyramid and approached her. Startled, she stood still, but there was little to frighten her any more. The worst had already happened. What, after all, could anyone do now except, perhaps, cut out her heart with a stone knife?

"Too late. Not walk here," said the shadow's voice. It was a gutteral voice, and almost as deep as her own.

"Ah, Señor Ruz. I don't mind the hour. It is very interesting by starlight. Can you tell me . . ."

"Too late," he said sharply. "There are snakes. Go back." A powerful arm took her elbow and turned her about. "I am responsible," he said. "Go home now."

To her astonishment, she found she was retracing her steps out to the road. Mr. Ruz followed behind her, not speaking, until they reached the entrance to the hotel. Then, as suddenly as he had appeared, he vanished into the black mass of the trees.

It was a novel experience for Mrs. Wagstaff to be sent home. But perhaps he was right. She was, she found, quite tired, and ready for bed. There was still a bit to read in her mystery, and she had promised it to the professor for the next day. If only the orgies next door could be silenced.

There was no need to worry. She could see, through the window next door, the still empty beds and a light in the bathroom. One of the girls was probably in . . . and one out? The silence was absolute, and lasted, as far as she was concerned, till the sun flickered through the vines onto her face next morning.

MRS. WAGSTAFF LAY AND GOT USED TO HERSELF FOR A while. It took some time, in the mornings, to recognize this heavy mountain entangled in the sheets. Somehow she always woke up feeling like the young, slim creature she had been when she married Gerald, and it took a little time to adjust. Getting up helped, of course, and getting into her corset, and piling her hair up neatly. By the time she had her dress and her powder on, she knew who she was again, and was not too dissatisfied. She could, since she accepted this self, enjoy the pleasures of food and drink, for instance . . . unlike her permanently dieting, irritable friends in Minneapolis.

It was quiet next door. Seven-fifteen. Not a time tourists woke up, but she had always been an early riser. Morning was a good time to explore, to get the feel of new places, before guides were about to drown you in information. Or, as often as not, misinformation. She struggled into a vast white cardigan, and then took it off. It was already warm. She put a black straw hat firmly on her piled hair . . . and let herself quietly out into the garden. Everything glistened. The grass was wet. A hummingbird darted and hung in an oleander bush. The scent of warm, green life was as dense as in a botanical garden hothouse. Down a winding side path she could see the white shirt of one of the gardeners. A little boy beside him was holding a tortilla in one hand and a yellow ball in the other. He looked up, saw Mrs. Wagstaff bearing down on him, grabbed to rescue the tortilla, and dropped the ball. It rolled to her large feet and he stared at it, frozen with dismay.

"Catch!" she directed, picking up the ball and throwing it overhand like a baseball pitcher. By some miracle, he reached up a hand and caught it. His face split open with glee, he stuffed the tortilla into his mouth and threw the ball back to her. She dropped her sack and caught it neatly. Not for nothing had she been shortstop for her college baseball team. They played concentratedly for five minutes, and might have gone on longer but the father, smiling widely, interrupted. "Sorry, Señora. He never want to stop." "Neither do I," she said. "Meet you here tomorrow," she told the boy and he beamed and nodded. She went on. There was no one else about.

The hotel dining room was silent, and there was no smell of coffee. She sighed. One trouble with being an early riser was that you could never get breakfast when you wanted it. It was one of the trials of travel that she was always hanging about waiting either for breakfast or for those unconscionably late continental dinners. Well, she had learned. Action was the thing. Fend off all thoughts of food. *Do* something.

She set off briskly down the road. It was a quiet, country place. The only house she passed was a hut surrounded by crooked palings. A white, embroidered huipil hung on a line near the door, and a cock was crowing somewhere. It was delightful to be alone on such a morning! She walked like a sergeant major, breathing deeply, enjoying the feel of her legs thrusting powerfully against the rank weeds on the edge of the road. She was at the entrance to the field of the great pyramid before she knew it. This time no Mr. Ruz appeared to deflect her. She came into the field and stood still. Great God, what a thing! Its shadow in the morning sun thrust itself halfway across the meadow, a strange, triangular darkness like nothing else she had ever seen. It was a great experience to feel so dwarfed. She was rarely dwarfed, she thought with a wry smile. It was good for the humility.

She walked all around Kukulcan's pyramid. All the explanations really did no good. How could one explain a human impulse that raised such a mountain of stone in order, apparently, that one could stand on top of it and cut out thousands of hearts with an obsidian knife! And then dismember the corpses and throw them down the other side! How explain those priests with their matted, bloody hair and robes, laboring to exhaustion at their ghoulish work? How explain such monsters who were also the most sophisticated mathematicians of their time? She stared up at the great flights of stairs. On the back flight there was not even a chain for the tourists to cling to, getting their pictures snapped. Probably in the great days, there were no chains. However did the people make it up and down without help? Perhaps the gods helped.

She wandered away across the field, looking back over her shoulder to astonish herself again at the mountain behind her. And as she glanced, the sun rose at last behind the pyramid and poured a great river of gold across the grass. A man was approaching down the road, his head up, staring, an open book in his hand. The tourists were waking up. She turned away briskly. She was certainly a typical tourist in this, at any rate: what she hated most was other tourists. The road from the field led through a silent woods full of shining spiderwebs. José hadn't mentioned it, but she knew this was a processional road. The Maya, brilliant as they were, had no wheeled vehicles. They didn't even use horses. There could be no other reason for so broad a road as this except for processions, religious, ceremonial crowds. The grass road was as broad as a city highway, and she followed it, to come out at last near the sacred well, the tarn, what they called a cenote.

Right on the tourist-tramped grass at the brink stood the remains of a stone house. She would have to ask José or Mr. Ruz about it. Was this where they had anointed the virgins? Did they burn incense at an altar here? Did anyone know . . . for sure?

She came up to the edge and looked down. There was sun dappling through the trees all about, but it seemed not to touch the black water of the cenote. She stared down into the opaque depths and thought of what still lay there in the ancient mud. An ugly thought. Then she looked across the pool to the other side. The wall of striated gray rock rose like a cliff to a sharp edge overhung with bushes. Nothing moved . . . not a leaf, not a bird. And then, something *did* move.

Her hand shielding her eyes from the sun, she gazed sharply across the water. Something flickered in the water near the opposite side. Something white. A sea gull? Surely too far inland. She stood like stone, peering. And then, slowly, she began to make her way along the edge, pushing through the vines and undergrowth. When she came, at last, to the other side she was moving with the speed of a charging rhinoceros, oblivious to the whiplashes on her hands and face. From directly above the spot, she looked down on what she had finally recognized.

A nude white body floated, almost motionless in the black water. Two small breasts moved gently, the nipples dimpling the surface. Something yellow as a spray of buttercups fanned out at one end, and under the buttercups, white as milk, a face looked up at her through the water.

WHEN SHE GOT BACK TO THE FIELD OF KUKULCAN, HER
breath was roaring like a lion in her chest. The man she had seen
was gazing up, the book still open in his hand. It was Mr. Moffatt,
alone for once, without his wife.

"You," she said, gasping. He turned, startled.

"You," she said again, breathing deeply three times as her yoga
exercises had taught her. "Go to the hotel and tell them there has
been an accident. In the cenote. Tell them to bring ropes." She
looked at his gray, bewildered face. "They'll need a grapple. For
God's sake, man, *go.* You can go faster than I can."

"Yes. Yes. of course. Could I do anything . . .?"

"Nothing to be done without ropes. Please go and tell them."

He started off at a trot. Then he looked back at her and began to
canter, his book flailing in his hand. Mrs. Wagstaff sat down on the
fourth step of the pyramid and waited.

She had had sparks of premonition for days. If only she had done
something, *said* something sooner, it might never have happened.
Obviously such a state of things must erupt. *Must.* And she had just

looked on, fascinated, as though it were all happening on a stage while she sat in the orchestra with no responsibility but to enjoy the show. Gerald was right. She *was* a nosy, interfering old trout. But if she was, she ought at least to make her interference *count.* Be of some *use!* She had just smiled . . . and now the poor child was dead!

She sat, a mountain of flesh on a mountain of stone, shaking her head like an angry bulldog, the contents of her bag slithered out along the step beside her. She sat until a stream of people erupted into the field and swarmed up to her.

Leading the way was the manager of the hotel, a dark man in an immaculate white shirt and a stiff collar. Beside him was José, a coiled rope and a metal hook over his shoulder, his face rigid as a poker. The professor was there and Mrs. Gibson and several of the gardeners and Mrs. Moffatt and Mrs. Crummit.

"What is it? Who's hurt?" demanded Mrs. Gibson. "Where?"

Mrs. Wagstaff rose, towering over them all. "At the cenote," she said, her oboe voice hoarse with anger. And they all made for the grassy road through the woods, Mrs. Crummit struggling to keep up. They were like a hive of bees as they went, but when they came out on the edge they fell silent, staring.

A strange sound came from someone, like a keening. It was José. Without a word, he started around the edge and they all followed, straggling through the bushes, peering down at the water, silent.

On the other side they stood where Mrs. Wagstaff had stood, numb, looking down. Mrs. Crummit began to whimper suddenly, and sat down hard on the grass, holding onto a bush as though she thought someone might push her into the well.

"My God," said Mrs. Gibson.

"She's tied!" said Professor Michelson. Most of his face was invisible under his beard, but his bald head was dappled red. "Here," he said, after a moment, in a voice he must have used on students, "let's get that grapple down."

The men swung the rope down over the side, reaching, groping for the rope that tied the wrists together. And again. And once more. Then the prongs caught and pulled the arms up. It looked as though the hook must pull them from their sockets.

"Wait," said Mrs. Wagstaff sharply. "Don't do that. Can't one of you go down the rope? Bring her up?" She turned to the men. "You, José, can't you go down?"

José turned to her a face of stone. "I?" He stared down at the white body, turning slightly at the end of the rope. "Yes. Yes, I will go."

They tied a length of rope under his arms and lowered him down the wall of the cenote. They lowered him until his legs hung in the water and he seemed standing beside her. He didn't move for a moment. Then he withdrew the prongs from her wrists and raised her body in the water with his arms. But he couldn't carry her that way, so he turned her like a package and put her over his shoulder, and they pulled him up.

When he laid her down on the grass, they stood in a silent ring about her. Barbara's golden hair streamed water. She stared up at them from wide, green eyes.

"She's alive," whispered Mr. Moffatt.

"No," said Mrs. Wagstaff. "It was the water that washed them open. She's dead." She looked at the limp, slight body, her own eyes as fierce as a hawk's. "Cut those ropes," she said. Mrs. Crummit had backed away, still sitting, her eyes horrified.

"No," said the manager. "We must call police. Nobody must touch."

"Yes," said Mrs. Wagstaff. "You are right." She reached into her enormous bag and rummaged. "Here," she said, pulling out a folded plastic raincoat. "I will cover her." She spread the bright green plastic over Barbara's body.

Instantly the soft, slim body was turned into a faceless mound. José gave a short, strangled sound and turned away into the bushes. The manager looked after him, startled. "Well," he said, after a moment, "someone must stay until police come."

One of the gardeners said something in rapid Spanish. "All right. He will stay. Please everyone to come away now."

"I will stay too," said Mrs. Wagstaff.

"Is no need," said the manager.

"I will stay," she repeated. "She was one of our group." How little she had been one of the group seemed now not important. This beautiful, imperious, silly child was dead. "You must tell the archaeology people. Her father. Dr. Canning, was to be back today."

"Oh, God," said Mrs. Gibson. "Who will tell him?"

"I will tell him." The professor's round, squirrel eyes were quiet, his voice heavy.

"You tell him," Mrs. Wagstaff said. "I will stay here." She sat down a little way from the body and stared across the water, her face as grim as death, doing, in some obscure way, penance for her sin of omission.

THE LOCAL POLICEMAN, A STOCKY, BULL-NECKED
little man, took over from Mrs. Wagstaff and the gardener in less
than an hour, but this was mañana country. It was afternoon before
a police detective arrived from Mérida to get things moving. By then
a solid phalanx of tourists stood in the open space near the ruined
stone building staring across the cenote at the white sheet that had
been draped over Barbara's body. They rustled like thirsty men
before a bar when the detective arrived, a hard-faced brown man
with a nose like a cockatoo. With him were Brian Bothwell and a tall,
thin man in rumpled white, his gray hair standing up in unkempt
wisps.

"It's her father," whispered one of the ladies. "Poor soul!" A sigh
of commiseration . . . and excited interest . . . went up from them.
They watched as the little group of men walked around the edge of
the cenote to the far side and stood beside the white heap. Suddenly, with a convulsive jerk, the old man leaned down and lifted
the sheet. Nobody breathed. Mrs. Wagstaff, who had remained with
the group of tourists, held her breath too. How could anyone hu-

man help it, she thought grimly. Brian looked, and turned abruptly away. Dr. Canning looked for what seemed ages. Then dropped the sheet, sat down heavily on the edge of the cenote, and dropped his head over his knees. The detective motioned to the policeman with him, and he lifted the white package that had been Barbara, and started to carry it around the edge. It seemed a slight effort. She had been a small girl. The tourists watched silently as the man came past and started down the processional road toward the field where the police car had been parked.

Mrs. Wagstaff sniffed, but neither in sorrow nor contempt. Something smelled odd. She looked down at the brown, trodden ground beside the stone ruins, but there was nothing there. She sucked the air in again. A funny, sweetish smell . . . like that store in Minneapolis that sold Indian brass and pot pipes. But there was no pipe here. Just a slightly sticky spot on the stone beside her, and the smell. Not marijuana. She knew that smell. She drew one sharp fingernail across the sticky spot and sniffed at it. That was it all right, but what was it? She shrugged. What difference did it make? Certainly none to that poor child.

"Poor child." The voice was like an echo out of her own head. Professor Michelson, his brown, sparking eyes for once somber, looked at her soberly. "She did not have a noble character, but it was not necessary that she go *that* way." He looked across at the men who still stood at the edge of the cenote. "It will be hard on her father."

"Yes." She stared at the man with a kind of anger. "Perhaps it should be. She could have used his attention . . . *before* this!"

"Yes. She was so—avid—for notice. Why do we never see these things in time?" He looked at Mrs. Wagstaff thoughtfully. "What you need . . . what, in fact, *we* need, is a good, big drink."

"At this hour? Surely the sun is not over the yardarm, professor."

"It is not the hour that counts. It is the occasion." He gestured with his head toward the cenote. "And this, I fear, is the occasion."

"You are quite right, Professor Michelson."

"I should prefer, Mrs. Wagstaff, that you call me Augustus. There is little point to formality after you have saved my life. You know, there is a theory that when you have saved someone's life, you are responsible for him forever." He smiled at her. "There is a thought to worry you!"

"I did nothing that vital, but I shall be glad to call you Augustus." Since he looked at her, evidently waiting, she added reluctantly, "My name is Elaine, and I am well aware that I am no lily maid of Astolat."

"That is fortunate. I always thought her a most insipid young woman."

They walked on. Whoever had brought Barbara to the pool must have come this way, she thought, but there were certainly no signs to be found on the trampled grass. The crowd had wiped out any marks, though for that matter, what signs could there be? It was only in detective stories that people were forever dropping unique shoe buckles or monogrammed handkerchiefs. Nowadays it was all Klee-nex—a most un-distinctive item. And there hadn't been any blood. Whoever the murderer had been, he had probably knocked her out, trussed her up, and flung her into the pool without dropping so much as a cigarette butt.

"Who was the malefactor?" asked Professor Michelson suddenly. They had come to the field, and he stopped to watch the policeman close the door to the back of the police car. The crowd had grown larger, despite the heat. "What is your opinion of *him*?" He jerked his beard toward the edge of the crowd where Mr. Cartwright stood stiffly, looking down at the ground.

"Why him?"

"I do not like to speak ill of the dead, you understand, but she *was*, as they say, giving him the business. What I mean is . . ."

"I know what you mean . . . Augustus. And you are quite right. She *was*. On the other hand, she was giving 'the business' to every-one, wasn't she?"

He looked at her with approving surprise. "Yes. quite. Everyone but me." He smiled ruefully. "I don't imagine she considered me an adequate challenge. Well. If not Mr. Cartwright, whom do you consider most likely?"

"Ourselves, perhaps? Either one of us is quite capable of killing someone in a totally locked room, are we not? We have had a good deal of literary experience of murder . . . and I have great confidence in the training powers of literature. In fact I am very tired of the kind of mystery in which a detective story writer attempting a *real* murder always turns out such a hopeless dud. *I* should certainly carry it off!"

"No doubt. No doubt. The problem in your case is motive. I can see no reason why you would have killed that child. Unless, perhaps, you were jealous of her and . . . Mr. Cartwright?"

"Why Cartwright? Why not José? or Mr. Bothwell? They are younger and more appealing, perhaps." Her broad face was as bland as a child's.

He cocked his head at her like a robin. "Perhaps so." He glanced over his shoulder to where the police detective, Brian Bothwell, and Dr. Canning were emerging from the processional road into the field. "Do you plan to tell the investigator about her . . . men?"

Her oboe voice grew darker. "That *does* seem . . . gratuitous."

"Well, I am for giving the detective the whole truth. In fiction, the great trouble for the police is less the murderer than it is other people's decision to conceal information . . . for a variety of stupid reasons. In *Death of a Hittite*, for instance, nothing would have happened to the hero at all if he had simply told the police his adventures at the beginning."

She smiled. "But then, you see, there would have been no book. I am quite willing to tell the whole truth. The question is, what *is* the whole truth? Is it indeed everything . . . facts, notions, speculations? I might as well accuse Susan. She is young and strong, and very jealous of her cousin! I have an idea we may be asked only for our facts. In that case, we can keep our speculations to ourselves." She looked up the dead, hot road toward the hotel. "Professor . . . Augustus . . . I think you are right." Her eyes were somber.

"Undoubtedly. But what about?"

"This *is* an occasion for a drink."

THE HOTEL HAD THE DISHEVELED LOOK OF A PLACE
where a great many servants have omitted to do their jobs. The
dining room was not cleared from lunch and the tiny waitresses
were buzzing at each other near the kitchen hatch. A heap of fresh
luggage stood in the hall, undistributed. No one had yet swept the
terrace floor. And a man who could have been nothing but a news-
paperman was having a quick one at the bar . . . and trying to pump
the bartender.

"Well, why *was* she with that bunch of old people if she was Dr.
Canning's daughter?" he was asking as Mrs. Wagstaff and the
professor came in.

The bartender, the same one who had been so avid for Barbara's
favor the night before, was reluctant to talk about it. He shrugged
and turned in relief to his new customers.

"Margarita?" asked the professor.

"No, I think not. Something with vodka, I think. A screwdriver?"

The reporter was eyeing them with great interest. "You from the

tour?" he asked brightly, having evidently forgotten his recent un-
complimentary noises about it.

"Yes, but we scarcely knew the girl," said Mrs. Wagstaff, to forestall him. Funny how reporters made people hold their tongues. All
that push and fervor dried up the springs of conversation. Even in
Yucatán, the reaction was the same.

"Is it true she was eviscerated?"

"E . . . what?" Little Mr. Gumbiner paused with a glass halfway to
his mouth.

Mrs. Wagstaff swung her head in despair. "No, no," she boomed.
"For goodness' sake, do not put that fable about. She was drowned."

The reporter, too pale to be Mayan, but too dark to be American,
looked disappointed. "Well, but drowned in the Virgin's Pool
wasn't she?"

"In the cenote, yes," agreed Mrs. Wagstaff.

"Tied up, I hear?"

"She'd have to be," Mr. Gumbiner cut in," wouldn't she? She
could swim like an eel."

"Ahh-ah," The reporter nodded with pleasure. It was clear he
could see the headlines: ACE SWIMMER MURDERED BY DROWNING. It
was not too bad a substitute for VIRGIN DROWNED IN VIRGIN POOL,
which was probably the other headline he had hoped for.

There was a sudden flurry at the door, and the Mérida detective
came in. Brian Bothwell was with him, his pale blue eyes flickering
and feverish in his thin, tanned face. Dr. Canning was not with them.

"I want to see everyone who was on the tour," said the detective.
His voice had a hard, gutteral twang, but it seemed to Mrs. Wagstaff
a little uncertain of itself. "Would you ask everyone, please, to come
into the lounge?"

"At once," the manager said, and sent three white-jacketed boys
scurrying.

They might all have been waiting, poised, for just this message,
so quickly did they filter in. The elderly, blue-haired ladies were full
of head-shaking distress . . . most of it the proper decorum for the
event. They hadn't like Barbara, and if they could have said what
was really in their minds, it would have been "served her right!"

Mrs. Crummit's dismay seemed more authentic. She looked shocked, even ill. Mrs. Gibson looked merely annoyed. One more irritation on a tour that wasn't giving them their money's worth. Mr. Cartwright was there alone. He moved with the jerkiness of an automaton and sat down on a hard chair against the wall, with no word to anyone. Mrs. Wagstaff, looking for reactions, didn't know what to make of his. He was like a man holding onto his control with white-knuckled tension. Why should he react so? Certainly Barbara had been outrageously cutting to him most of the time. Except for the unsettling few times she had used him sweetly as a pawn in her other games. Was he broken up? Or conscience-stricken? Or sick to his stomach? It was hard to tell from his stiff, red face.

Susan was a surprise too. She came hurrying in, her face white, but tearless. Her hair swirled over her shoulders in a beautiful black torrent . . . and she was wearing, *surely* she was wearing lipstick?

Last of all, there were voices in the hall and then José and Señor Ruz came in. They too, it seemed, were to be considered part of the tour. The curious thing—the tragic thing—Mrs. Wagstaff thought, was that nobody looked heartbroken. Even the men who had seemed to care, even her fiancé, looked overwrought, *shocked* rather than wretched.

"Thank you, ladies and gentlemen." The detective looked them all over from mud-brown eyes. "I am Inspector Molo. I wish to say that the police are now in charge of this most tragic affair. I do not wish to interfere with your vacation trip, but you understand that there is a murderer to be apprehended." He sounded surprised and a little pleased with the felicity of his last phrase. Professor Michelson looked at Mrs. Wagstaff significantly, and waggled his caterpillar eyebrows up and down. They had had several discussions about whether or not policemen were too often made inept in the books.

"There is much to do today, so I will not detain you now. I wish only to say that we are on the job, and that I must ask you all to remain available here until I have a chance to talk to you."

"In this *room?*" asked Mrs. Gibson sharply.

"No, no. I mean not to leave Chichén Itzá." Lieutenant Molo

looked harried . . . and hurried. "I will try to talk to you later . . . this evening, or tomorrow morning. Now, if you will . . ."

"Why not now?" The words came in an explosive burst. They all turned to stare at Mr. Cartwright. Mrs. Crummit jumped nervously, and seized Mrs. Bernardi's arm.

"Not time now," said the Lieutenant. "Please, just do not leave this area. Stay near the hotel."

"How long?" Mrs. Gibson was not to be put off.

"Until I have time!" The lieutenant's voice was sharp.

"He is a traffic cop!" whispered Professor Michelson to Mrs. Wagstaff.

Lieutenant Molo turned abruptly, and followed by a tiny policeman, was gone.

"Well!" said Mrs. Gibson. "It was hardly worth our coming here just to hear *that!*" She looked curiously at Mr. Cartwright. "Of course," she said, "*I* have nothing to tell him, but you'd think he'd be interested in those who *do!*"

"Don't worry," said Mr. Gumbiner. "He'll get to that. Maybe he's got to get an autopsy, or something. It's kind of a *hot* country, ye know, and . . ." His voice trailed off into the horrified silence.

Bothwell wheeled suddenly about and disappeared out the terrace door. José looked at the gaggle of ladies in his care, his dark eyes darting from one to the other. "Ladies," he said, "please do not be upset. If you will go now to your cottages, I'm sure all will be taken care of soon. Please?"

The ladies were herded out, and followed by José and the totally impassive mahogany man that was Señor Ruz. Mrs. Wagstaff remained, staring thoughtfully at her solid brogues.

"Will you join me in another drink, Elaine?" The professor's brown eyes crinkled at her out of the furry nest of his beard, and his bald head shone. "I am in need of some opinions other than my own."

She nodded. "Yes. I don't know what that man has in mind, but it seems to me a mistake not to talk to everyone first. What do you suppose Mr. Cartwright had to tell him?"

Professor Michelson ordered their drinks, and gazed judiciously at his joined fingertips. "That he killed her? That he *saw* who killed her? That he knew something suspicious about one of us?"

"Any one of those, I expect. I wonder . . ."

"What do you wonder?"

"Who could have hated her enough to kill her."

"Any one of our ladies. They all dislike her . . . for obvious reasons."

"Yes, but that is dislike you are talking about. I am talking about *hate*. One does not kill a girl of eighteen from dislike. And in any case, this is not the kind of murder done by old ladies." She gazed at the professor blandly. "They are a fragile bunch . . . with the exception of myself. And *I* didn't even dislike her."

"Nor I."

"No. A good point. I think men would not dislike her. They would either hate her or love her. And perhaps both at once. She could be quite maddening to the male, I suspect. Would you care to corroborate that for your sex?"

He laughed. "It isn't often I get the chance to speak for my sex. But yes, I think she inspired more active feelings in men than dislike."

11

WHEN THEY HAD CHEWED OVER THEIR THOUGHTS, MRS.
Wagstaff and the professor parted to return to their cottages. The
garden was deserted, green, and somnolent in the sunlight. The
pool lay blue and still as she went past it. She looked at it curiously.
Odd that Barbara hadn't been found *there.* It was certainly quiet and
secluded enough at night . . . and surely a lot more convenient than
the cenote. And how had she been taken there? It was a long walk
if you had to carry a body . . . even a light body. And if the girl had
been killed *at* the cenote itself, how had she happened to *be* there?
She was certainly no archaeology buff who would conceivably wander off *that* distance for sheer love of research. Well then, if she had
not been killed elsewhere and carried there, she must have gone
with someone. Who would she have gone with? Mrs. Wagstaff remembered the dining room when she had left it the night before.
Barbara had been with Brian Bothwell then. But that proved nothing. She had probably not been killed till much later. She might have
met someone after everyone else had gone to bed. Mrs. Wagstaff
sighed irritably. Why hadn't she been on deck last night, as she had

the night before when she had seen Barbara in the swimming pool? An interesting scene, that. Either José or the strange Mr. Ruz looked capable of murdering her.

Mrs. Wagstaff walked slowly around the pool, looking into the clear, blue depths. Down the little side path from the diving board was the Cartwrights' cottage. They had one to themselves, perhaps because she was an invalid. Mrs. Wagstaff looked at the pretty, vine-draped, silent cottage and then, on an impulse, turned and walked down the path. Where was Mrs. Cartwright? She had not been at dinner the night before, nor had she seen her today.

The door of the cottage was closed. She had raised her hand to knock, when she realized how futile that gesture was. If Mrs. Cartwright were there alone . . . and she hadn't seen *him* come back . . . she couldn't answer a knock. She lowered her hand slowly. There was a window beside the door, and without pausing to consider how unladylike the action was, she bent to look in. What she saw was a room just like her own, twin beds, a little table with a lamp, an open closet door, a sweater lying on a chair. But the shock was Mrs. Cartwright. She sat in her wheelchair, her back to the door, motionless. Mrs. Wagstaff couldn't think for a moment why she felt such a chill at the sight. And then she realized. Mrs. Cartwright's back was to the door and to the window onto the garden. The view was all behind her, where she could not see it. In front of her was a blank wall and the open closet. She must have been sitting there like that all the afternoon. He must have left her like that . . . and she couldn't move!

She tapped at the door abruptly, and went in. Mrs. Cartwright's head quivered, but she did not turn.

Mrs. Wagstaff went up and stood by the closet door where she could be seen. The anguish in the large, gray eyes was so stark that Mrs. Wagstaff drew in her breath sharply.

"Are you all right?"

The gray eyes stared for a moment and then slowly closed and opened again. She could not speak, but the message was clear. Yes, I am all right.

But no, clearly she wasn't. Oh, physically there seemed to be no catastrophe, but that first look was not to be erased from Mrs. Wagstaff's mind. She wished fiercely that she had, in these ten days of the trip, made some effort to approach this woman. She knew, after all, nothing about her except her affliction. To be afflicted is to be alone. Everyone, of course, is alone, but the blind, the dumb, the paralyzed, are set apart in a special isolation. It is hard enough to get close to ordinary people. The effort to reach the special, the maimed, is too much for most people to make, so they live in a kind of limbo outside of life.

There was nothing wrong with this woman's mind. In this numb, dead body the brain ticked on and on, helpless even to shut itself off.

Mrs. Wagstaff turned the wheelchair around toward the garden window. "Can I get you something?" she said. "Have you had lunch?"

The gray eyes closed and opened. Yes. Someone . . . Mr. Cartwright? . . . had fed her, and then left her like that. Had he told her anything? Did she even know what had happened?

"Did Mr. Cartwright tell you? Was he here?"

The lids drew down over the gray eyes. Yes, he had been here, but a small frown grew between the fine brows, a question. So she didn't know. He had not, for some reason, told her.

"I suppose you'll have to know," Mrs. Wagstaff said slowly. "Last night Barbara Canning . . . the blonde girl, you know . . . was— killed. I found her this morning, in the cenote."

The gray eyes grew round with shock, and the wailing, loon cry came suddenly from her mouth. One delicate hand scrabbled convulsively on the arm of the wheelchair. Mrs. Wagstaff put a large hand on her shoulder and squeezed the frail bones comfortingly. Mrs. Cartwright grew still, but her eyes traveled wildly about the room and settled at last on a chair. Mrs. Wagstaff turned to look.

There was nothing to be seen but a blue, wool sweater draped over the seat. A man's sweater.

Mrs. Cartwright stared at the chair a long moment and then her eyes closed and did not open. She shivered under Mrs. Wagstaff's hand.

"What is it?" Mrs. Wagstaff asked, but she was talking to herself. She sat down in front of the wheelchair. "You must not be upset," she said in her deepest oboe tones. "The police will find out who did it. They are working . . ."

The door smacked open without warning. Mrs. Wagstaff turned to look over her shoulder at the tall figure silhouetted against the green of the garden.

"Can I do something for you, Mrs. Wagstaff?" Mr. Cartwright looked at her with obvious hostility.

She rose. "No. I think not. I was visiting with your wife." She paused and looked at the dark eyes on a dead level with her own. "She had not heard about Miss Canning."

"So you thought you'd better tell her," he said harshly.

"It did not seem likely that she could be kept in ignorance. I have no doubt Lieutenant Molo will wish to see her tomorrow."

"I doubt that. There is nothing she could tell him." He spoke of her—they *both* did—she thought painedly—as though she were not there. "Now if there is nothing I can do for you, I trust you will forgive me if I attend to my wife. I have been called away too long already."

"Quite so. She was sitting facing the wall!" She moved around to where Mrs. Cartwright could see her. "I'll come in to see you again if I may," she said. The gray eyes closed and opened. Yes. But she looked exhausted . . . and frightened.

Why was she frightened? Mrs. Wagstaff, who did not often kick herself, felt like doing so now. She had been wrong to tell the poor creature about Barbara. What good could it do to upset her? It had not occurred to her that Mrs. Cartwright's immobility made her peculiarly susceptible to fear. Anyone, after all, could do anything to her. She thought, suddenly, of the day before at the cenote. Surely she had been terrified. Surely she, Elaine Wagstaff, had not just dreamed that Mr. Cartwright had let go of her chair momentarily? Was he a sadist then? Or was a vista of years with such an invalid sometimes too much to bear? Was he a monster . . . or a poor, miserable wretch? Certainly he was not the saint they had all comfortably thought him. He *had* left his wife alone to stare at the wall. And what had so frightened her about the chair in her room?

Mrs. Wagstaff paused with one hand on the doorjamb of her own cottage and stared unseeingly at the sunlit purple bougainvillea. She tried to remember what had been said just before. It was, wasn't it, just after she had told her about Barbara? What did Barbara have to do with that chair? It was a quite ordinary chair with a sweater tossed casually over it. A man's sweater. Mr. Cartwright's sweater. So what? She walked into her room, swabbing her broad face with a handkerchief. The afternoon sun was like a sauna bath. She took off her shoes, groaning a little, and stretched out on the bed. In a moment she had stuck to it, the back of her dress moist and adhesive. It was no climate for a sweater.

She lay limply for a moment. Suddenly she sat up straight. That was it! That sweater. No one in his right mind could wear a sweater in this heat. Even in the morning it was too warm for wool sweaters. There was only one time when sweaters made any sense . . . and that was late at night, when things had cooled off. But at dinner Mr. Cartwright had been wearing only pants and a light sport shirt. So . . . unless that sweater had been lying there for days . . . and that was unlikely with the maids in every day except today—he had worn it last night. Late last night. Certainly after dinner. So he had gone out sometime in the evening, leaving his wife in the cottage . . . alone.

WHY, MRS. WAGSTAFF ASKED HERSELF ACIDLY, WHY . . . IF you have to be a busybody . . . can't you manage to be one at a useful time . . . such as the night someone gets killed? Why, on that of all nights, must you take a tepid little walk, get marched home by a guide, and go spinelessly to bed?

The question was, should she find Lieutenant Molo and give him her tiny parcel of information? She stood in front of her bathroom mirror and questioned her vast image. What could she tell him? Mr. Cartwright was out late last night. So what? Perhaps he would tell that himself. Besides, lots of people were probably out last night. Anyhow, how do you know? Because I saw a sweater on a chair in his cottage. What does *that* prove? Nothing, by itself, but you should have seen his wife's expression! Really, Mrs. Wagstaff, might I suggest that you are wasting our valuable time with foolish imaginings? But . . . but . . . thank you, Mrs. Wagstaff, now if you'll close the door behind you. . . . She could see that as a scenario for her chat with Lieutenant Molo. He didn't look like a man who suffered fools gladly.

On the other hand, this might be IT. The clue. Mr. Cartwright, after all, was so likely a candidate for chief murderer. Hell hath no terrors like a man whose ego has been wounded. Perhaps, though, it would be wiser to prowl about on her own and get some more substantial evidence. Men were such prisoners of the fact! They were so rarely subtle enough to function on insight. She sighed massively and dabbed her face with the warm water in the pitcher. Even Gerald, impressed as he was with her batting average of right assumptions, was forever demanding substantiating facts. He was uneasy relying on psychology and intuition. And because the world was run so largely by men, most institutions and techniques were geared to *their* ways. Very few companies, courts, colleges, were run on the basis of hunches, quivers in the shoulder blades, psychological recognitions, *feelings* . . . but who is to say that the fact should be king, that it is always so much smarter than a quiver?

As far as she was concerned, a man who could leave his wife staring at the wall for hours was capable of anything. She dried her face gently, so as not to produce a new burst of perspiration. The thing to do was not to talk to Molo, but to try to find out who had seen Mr. Cartwright last night, and when was the last time anyone had seen Barbara?

She put her shoes back on, went out and down a path, and knocked smartly at the professor's cottage door. He came to the door in his socks. White socks. "Ah. Elaine," he said brightly. "Will you come in? I've been reading *The Turn of the Screw,* a quite extraordinary work. James has been underestimated as a mystery writer, don't you think?"

"Quite. I won't come in, but would you care for a stroll about the grounds?" She looked significantly at the door beside his. Mrs. Gibson was on the other side of his wall . . . and the walls, as she knew, were like paper.

"Certainly." He turned the corner of his page down in most unscholarly fashion, slipped into his shoes, and came out. They strolled. He looked at her face. "What is bothering you, perturbed spirit?" he said.

"I am concerned about Mrs. Cartwright," she said.

"Mrs? I, on the other hand, am concerned about Mr. Cartwright."

"It's the same thing, I suspect. What is your point?"

"He purports to be that saintly figure, the man devoted to a crippled wife, doing all for her . . . and yet clearly overheated about a girl half his age. Ever since I read *As a Matter of Corpse* I have been suspicious of noble characters. In that book . . ."

"I know it," she interrupted. "And I agree. It has never seemed to me that nobility in man is a frequent quality . . . and it is certainly very often a faked one." She told him the story of Mr. Cartwright's sweater.

"She was frightened, was she?" he said thoughtfully. "Poor soul."

"I'm not sure whether she was afraid *of* him or afraid *for* him. Anyway, I'd guess he was out last night. You didn't, by any chance, see him, did you?"

"As a matter of fact, I *did.* I came out around ten to get a breath of air, and he was just starting down the drive. He walked out to the road. As soon as I saw him bend his steps toward the pyramid, I went the other way. He is not exactly the companion I would choose for an evening stroll."

"But he was alone?"

"Yes. He stepped along rather fast, but he was alone." A frown drew his furry brows into a deep vee over his eyes. "Could he have been following Barbara at that time? If I had only gone with him, do you suppose I could have . . ."

"Who knows? Did he see you?"

"I don't think so. I was walking on the grass . . . and I was, shall we say, evading his company."

"When was the last time anyone saw Barbara?"

"That's the kind of question the police should be asking us all. What *are* they doing, do you suppose?"

She shrugged her shoulders and dropped her bag on the path. The flashlight and a pink rain hat dribbled out the end of it. The professor bent to pick them up and she regarded the top of his bald head with grave interest.

"I should suggest you wear a hat," she said. "You are getting dangerously sunburned."

"Oh?" He promptly clapped the rain hat on his head, his beard foaming out from under its pink brim. "May I?"

She smiled. "Please do. It is most becoming. Now, where were we? Oh, yes, who saw Barbara last?"

"I saw her at dinner, and not thereafter. But there is no way to find out without questioning everyone on the tour."

"Not to speak of outsiders . . . like Bothwell, José, Señor Ruz, the young bartender . . . nor tramps, nor local fanatics."

"Why don't you ask your cottage mate? Young Susan probably knows more of her comings and goings than anyone else. If you recall, in *Corpus Derelicti* it was the paid companion who had the key clue."

Mrs. Wagstaff shuddered suddenly. "And if *you*, recall," she said somberly, "she got killed because of it."

WHEN MRS. WAGSTAFF GOT BACK TO HER COTTAGE, IT was almost five. Susan was sitting on the verandah bench looking freshly washed, cool, and tense. Mrs. Wagstaff came up and put a hand on her shoulder.

"I *am* sorry about your cousin," she said. "It is hard to believe, isn't it?"

The girl's fine, brown eyes brimmed suddenly with tears. "I really *don't* believe it! And I'm so *awful!*"

"Now you're at it again. Self-denigration is a waste of living time. You can't always be in the wrong, my dear. *Why* are you so awful?"

Susan wiped her face with the back of her hand and looked out over the garden. "Because I can't really care!" The words burst from her like a hand grenade. "And poor Uncle Larry is so broken up. And I *was* supposed to be sort of her chaperone. I didn't do much of a job, did I?" Her lips trembled, and she drew them in fiercely.

"Well, you couldn't exactly follow her around, could you? Did she ask you to go out with her last night?"

She laughed bitterly. "That's a funny idea! She wouldn't be caught dead in the evening with *me* in tow!" She gasped as she heard what she had said.

"Well, then, there's nothing much you could have done. Did she disappear right after dinner?"

"No. She went somewhere with Brian, but then she came back later by herself. I thought she was going to stay in for once." She gulped. "She stayed in just long enough to borrow my perfume and do over her face."

"Was Brian waiting for her somewhere?"

"I don't know. I don't think so. She was kind of giggly, as if she was up to something. I asked her when she'd be back . . . and all she'd say was not to wait up for her!" She wiped her face vigorously with the back of her arm, and Mrs. Wagstaff looked up to see Brian Bothwell coming down their path. His face was taut. He looked strung up tight as a bomb.

"I've got to go up to the dig to be with Uncle Larry," Susan said. She stared up at Mrs. Wagstaff. "I don't know what to *say* to him!"

"As little as possible," Mrs. Wagstaff advised." Just put your arms around him and hug him. Sometimes that's enough."

"Hug Uncle *Larry?*

"Why not? All of us need touching now and then."

"I suppose so. It's just that Uncle Larry is so . . . remote." She stood up. "Hello, Brian. I'm ready . . . I guess."

"Right. Let's go." He turned away from Mrs. Wagstaff after one short, blank nod, but then he turned back suddenly. "Are they questioning anyone yet?" he asked.

"I don't think so," Mrs. Wagstaff answered." I don't know what the lieutenant is doing, but nobody has been called in yet. Perhaps we will be tomorrow."

"I should think so," he said hoarsely. "I should think so."

She watched them walk away together, he stalking, thin and wordless, beside her. Well, she thought, it doesn't look very promising for Susan at the moment. But of course it's still early days. He may come around yet, after the shock wears off.

She went into her room, sat down, and picked up her book. Stephen's *Incidents of Travel in Central America, Chiapas and Yucatan* was a fascinating account of this very area, and she was getting very knowledgeable about such things as milpa culture and the invasion of Yucatán by the Itzás. But right here, on the very ground, it seemed fatuous to sit in one's room and *read* about it. She tossed the book down on the bed and looked out. The sun was still shining, but it was not quite so hot. She would go and look at the ruins. She *was*, after all, here to *see* things. No use being a lugubrious hypocrite about it. Furthermore, this was a good time to evade both tourists and guides. The tourists would be indoors for drinks and rests before dinner, and the guides would go wherever guides went. A bit of a mystery, that. Did they just disappear into rock fissures when the tourists were safely bedded down, or did they go into the village for gaiety with the local natives? José didn't seem quite up to gaiety, but who knew?

She did meet a group of tourists on the road, returning from the field. Señor Ruz was with them . . . and they seemed not to have any other guide. A second-class tour, she thought wryly. They had to hire someone on the spot, instead of being accompanied by someone like José. Señor Ruz, if her experience was any sample, would not be of great informational value to these people. However, at the moment information was the last thing they wanted. They were hot, dusty-looking, and tired. They had that "tourists at five o'clock look" recognizable all over the world.

She nodded at Señor Ruz as she passed, but he was as impassive as ever.

A small lamppost marked the entrance to the field, and she paused by it to lean over and tie a shoelace. When she stood up again she looked over toward the great pyramid, the focus of the empty field. The sun was low now and cast a long shadow, but on the far side of the pyramid someone bent low to the ground as if also tying a shoelace. She walked through the gate, idly wondering who her echo was. Whoever it was crouched a singularly long time for such a minor chore. Perhaps he had dropped something. As she came closer, it became clear that it *was* someone searching, a man. He moved slowly, his head bent to the ground, like a questing bird dog. And then, suddenly, he seemed to glance up and see her approaching. With eerie speed, he ducked down by the shadowed base of the pyramid as if he had fallen flat on the ground.

This was too much for Mrs. Wagstaff. She had no objections to secrets, but she didn't believe in secrets from *her*. Someone didn't want to meet her. With determined speed, she strode across the dry grass to the corner of the pyramid. When she rounded it, she stopped in surprise. Mr. Cartwright was standing there, looking up at the pyramid.

"Have you lost something, Mr. Cartwright?" she asked.

His face was so brick red that she feared he might be apoplectic . . . probably the effect of leaning over so long.

"Uh . . . yes," he said. "My pen. It dropped out of my pocket somewhere hereabouts."

"Oh, what a nuisance," she said. "My husband was always bending over and losing things out of his shirt pockets. Now I always carry a bag." She looked at her gunny sack complacently. "Can I help you look?"

"No," he said shortly, and then, as if remembering her age and sex, "thank you. It's not here. I shall give it up. I just thought it was worth a try." He nodded at her and started past.

"Well, if I find it, I'll bring it back for you," she said. He went on abruptly toward the gate.

Now what was he really looking for, she wondered, watching him. Pen indeed. More likely some telltale clue he had left when he killed Barbara! She looked down at her feet and walked slowly the great length of the pyramid's base. She *did* find an American dime, but that was too anonymous to be a clue. The dry, tufty grass had nothing more to offer. She wandered off across the field toward the processional road. She had no desire to go down it again to that grim, stone tarn, but she was drawn irresistibly to that edge of the field. When she got to the place where the grass road opened through the trees, she peered down it and got her second surprise. Men were bent over, like Mr. Cartwright, searching the road. There were three of them, in khaki uniforms, and Lieutenant Molo stood nearby, watching them. This, evidently, was what seemed to him more important than talking to all the tour people. Perhaps he was right . . . though she doubted it. Maybe it was necessary to find what clues there were before nightfall, or before the murderer could return to correct his errors.

"Well," she said to him, "are you finding whatever you are looking for? This does seem to be a day for searching."

He looked at her sharply. "Why do you say that?" he asked.

She was offhand. "Nothing in particular. Mr. Cartwright was just looking for his fountain pen, and your men seem busily engaged."

"Mr. Cartwright? Where? When?"

"Over by the pyramid, where he thought he'd dropped it. He didn't find it." She looked at him innocently. "Have *you* found it perhaps?"

"No." she saw with some satisfaction that he was irritated and suspicious. "We have found nothing. Nothing. I have not enough men!"

Always one to risk a rebuff, Mrs. Wagstaff stuck her broad neck out. "What are you looking for?"

It was clear he would have preferred not to answer, but Mrs. Wagstaff was not easily to be ignored. "Something," he said briefly, "anything. To show who carried Miss Canning this way."

"Carried? Are you sure she didn't walk?"

"We are sure," he said, "of nothing. Mrs———?"

But they were interrupted. One of the men made a sudden exclamation and stood up, palm outstretched.

Lieutenant Molo went up to him to see, and Mrs. Wagstaff followed. The object on the man's outstretched hand was familiar to her. It was part of a wooden earring, carved like a serpent.

"That's Barbara's earring," she said. "She bought them at the bazaar in Mérida a few days ago."

The lieutenant swung around as if he had forgotten her. "Oh? You identify this object? It is of a certainty Miss Canning's?"

"Yes, I'm quite sure. She was intrigued by all the snake ornaments, and she showed her new earrings around." She shivered slightly, looking at the twined wooden snake with the reared head, and recalling it hanging from Barbara's tiny ear. "Not that it helps much, I suppose," she said. "She must have come along here some-how. You know that already. What you need is a clue to the *man.*"

His flat brown eyes glinted. "Or woman," he said.

"Woman? I should hardly think a woman could carry her so far."

"There are strong women," he said noncommittally, but his eyes raked her massive shoulders. "Miss Canning was very small."

"What makes you think she was carried? Perhaps she walked there with someone . . . all the way."

"That is conceivable." He looked at the broken earring in his hand. "This earring says nothing. It could just have fallen off in either case."

Mrs. Wagstaff looked at the piece again. It wasn't really broken, she noticed. It was just detached from its backing. It would have taken a sharp jerk to do that. "Wait," she said slowly. "She *was* carried."

"What? How do you know that?" His eyes narrowed in his dark face.

"I just remembered something. Her ears were pierced. In ordi-nary use, the earring would never have come apart like that. Some-thing must have pulled it. If she were carried and the earring caught in a bush or something, the wooden part might have pulled off the backing. The whole thing couldn't have come away because it was fastened *through* her earlobe. And it wouldn't have fallen off if she were just walking."

The lieutenant's beaked nose pointed at her. "You are certain that her ears were pierced?"

"Yes. She kept telling Susan—that is her cousin—to get hers done too. It was so convenient."

"That is easy to verify, of course, from the body." He would obviously take nothing from her as gospel.

"Of course," she agreed gravely.

He stared at her a moment, his hand closing over the earring.

"Mrs . . . Wigstaff? Since you are here, perhaps you would tell me your opinion of the relations between this young woman and the men of the tour. Who hated her?"

"Ah," she said. "If it is hate you mean, I can't say for sure. Most of the women disliked her."

"Why was that?"

"She was a considerable beauty. And she was not fond of women."

"Yes. But hate, that is a different matter."

She looked at him with interest. He was not totally a traffic cop. "Yes. The men were all interested. And competitive. She played them off against each other."

"That is a dangerous practice. Who, of the men, would you say was most ... disturbed?"

She shrugged her broad shoulders. "That is hard to say. The guide, José, was quite smitten. Mr. Cartwright was certainly intrigued. Mr. Bothwell was, perhaps, engaged to her."

"So he has said. He is considerably ... disturbed."

"But my comments are all hearsay. It could be someone quite unconnected with the tour. Someone local? Someone insane? Someone who tried to assault her? *Was* she assaulted?" The idea had just occurred to her.

"You are asking more questions than you are answering," said the inspector.

She had a vivid memory of Barbara in the swimming pool, and her wet, angry face as she ran by, pulling up her bikini. "*Was* she assaulted?"

"I cannot tell you that. The medical examiner has not finished. Now, will you tell me something?"

"Certainly."

"Where were *you* last evening?"

"At what time was she killed?"

He looked at her frigidly. "Would you answer the question please?" She smiled. "I haven't much of an alibi."

"Oh?"

"After dinner I went for a walk by myself. Then I came home and went to bed." She pushed her lower lip out judicially. "Not a very stimulating evening."

"And you did not meet or talk to anyone? To Miss Canning, for instance?"

"Not Miss Canning. I saw Mr. Ruz in the pyramid field and he suggested I should go home because there were snakes."

"Quite true. What was he doing there?"

"I have no idea. Perhaps he was organizing his lecture for today. He is our ruins guide, you understand."

"Yes, I know. And you never saw Miss Canning after dinner?"

"No."

"Was she quite as usual at dinner?"

Mrs. Wagstaff thought of Barbara at dinner, her jabs at Mrs. Crummit, her seesaw reaction to Brian Bothwell, her sudden interest in Ruz and Cartwright.

"Yes," she said, "I should say very much as usual."

He looked at her darkly, his nose elevated, as if he were sniffing for another question. He did not seem to find any.

"All right," he said dismissingly, and turned away from her. She looked after him. She had lost all taste for ruins now, and it was getting shadowy. Still, since she was here, she might as well take a quick look at the temple of the warriors.

"Oh, Mrs. Wigstiff!"

She looked back at him. It was idle to correct her name. "Yes?"

"Do not remain here alone. Whoever killed Miss Canning is not in custody . . . yet."

The remark sent an interesting tingle up her back, the sort of tingle she had used to have from Gerald. He was probably right, but she could think of no reason for anyone to murder *her*. People *did* murder young girls like Barbara, and sometimes helpless old ladies with money, but she fitted into no such category. She was not, she considered, a murderee type. Still . . .

"Yes. Thank you," she said. "I will just take a look at the warrior temple and go back to the hotel."

She walked along briskly until she came to the great, curious temple of the warriors. It was a fantastic place—a building surrounded on two sides by rows and rows of columns, hundreds of columns, about six feet high, which simply stood there, supporting nothing. It was hard to imagine what they could have been for. In front was a Chac Mool, a stone figure of a man lying on his back with raised knees and a bowl on his stomach. She walked around slowly, looking at it. Nobody seemed sure what these figures were for. Offerings? A seat? An altar?

All at once the silence of the columns, the enigma of the Chac Mool invaded her. No one could know anything of these people except what they could deduce from these ruins. Nothing was left of their speech, few hints about their language. After that fanatical monk Diego de Landa had finished burning all the Mayan manuscripts because they were *evil,* that is to say, *non-Christian,* there was nothing left but three enigmatic books found years later in Europe. And these had not been deciphered. So here it was, this incomparable, ferocious civilization that had produced incredible architecture, science, and art . . . but had no tongue to tell of it, no words to speak. Mayan ruins were like a great genius . . . who was mute.

The shadows were long now, laying down a series of dark fingers from the forest of columns. It was still. Ominously still. She jumped when a bird called. She looked about at the stark columns, the coiling stone serpents everywhere. No one had lived here for hundreds of years, but there were ugly vibrations in the air. It was a dark place, a place where one would not be surprised to find a young girl, naked and bound, floating in a well.

WHEN MRS. WAGSTAFF CAME THROUGH THE HOTEL AND crossed the terrace to go back to her cottage, a dark figure rose from a small table by the parapet. A froth of beard thrust out at her. "Ah, Elaine," said Professor Michelson. "Come relax a moment before dinner."

"I'm a dusty mess," said Mrs. Wagstaff. "I should go and clean up before dinner."

He cocked his head at her consideringly. "Change nothing," he said. "You look perfectly soignée."

Mrs. Wagstaff snorted . . . but gently. Nobody since Gerald died had noticed or remarked on how she looked. And nobody could *ever* have thought her soignée. It was the curse of getting old. *One* of the curses. Old ladies spent infinite time on their hair, their nails, their jewelry, and their clothes . . . and nobody cared.

"Well," she said, settling into a chair with a vast creak of her underpinning, "If I am that elegant, I had better not spoil the effect. And I *should* like to talk to you."

"Good. Somehow I feel that if we could really pool our knowledge and our experience, we could solve this tragedy ourselves. Frankly—" his bald head glimmered in the moonlight—"I've just about decided the murderer has to be Cartwright."

"Ah. That is most interesting. You may be interested to know that I saw him this afternoon, looking for something near the pyramid."

He whistled softly. "The clue! He must have followed Barbara. That must have been where he was going so fast when I saw him last night! And he killed her near the pyramid. But in his hurry, he dropped something there and didn't find it out until today. So he was searching. It makes a kind of ghastly sense."

"There's one trouble with that hypothesis, Augustus."

"Oh? What?"

"If he was going after her, who was Barbara *with?* It's not likely that she went down there alone."

"That's easy. She was going to meet *him,* and she was a little ahead of him!"

She shook her head at him. "No. Not from what Susan said. She came back in, got herself fixed up and went out again . . . but she was excited, mischievous, *up* to something!"

"Well, if she was going off to meet a married man, that would account for it, wouldn't it?"

"Perhaps. I just don't seem to connect her giggling excitement with a meeting with Mr. Cartwright. But . . . you could be right. She could have thought it would be amusing to lead him on." A streak of distaste flitted across her face. It was true that the girl would not have thought twice about such a maneuver. It had all the qualities she most enjoyed . . . making a fool of one man and making another man jealous, or *two* other men, for where was José while all this was going on . . . and where was Bothwell?

"What I don't understand," said the professor with a wriggle of annoyance, "is why he went to all that trouble? He could have knocked her out in the garden and thrown her into the swimming pool not fifty feet from his cottage. Then he could have whipped indoors and nobody the wiser. *Mrs.* Cartwright couldn't inform on him. Why go all the way to the field? Why, for that matter, drown her in so . . . aboriginal a way?"

"Yes. That *is* the puzzle. Why . . ." She stopped short. Footsteps came cracking across the terrace and a tall, dark figure ran hastily down the steps. Mr. Cartwright was on his way home! They sat quite still in the darkness and watched him emerge from the dim path, circle the swimming pool, and descend toward his cottage.

Professor Michelson let his breath out noisily. "Well! I still think he's the most likely one to . . ."

The sound made Mrs. Wagstaff's hair stir on her head. The professor, who had no hair to react, gulped in his words. It was a ululation, a weird, inhuman cry, wild as a loon's.

"What *is* it?" the professor whispered hoarsely.

She listened, but the sound was not repeated. "I don't know. Wait. Yes, I do. It's Mrs. Cartwright."

She rose from her chair.

"Where are you going?"

"I want to see what the trouble is."

He walked beside her like an eager terrier. "You are planning to look in the window?"

"No. I'm going to pay a call. You had better go home, Professor."

"No, no. I shall wait for you. There may be trouble." He sounded worried. For *her!* "I shall accompany you," he said firmly.

"Nonsense! I won't be long. Wait for me, if you like." It was rather comforting to see him sitting beside the pool as she surged down the path to the cottage.

For a moment there was utter stillness in response to her knock.

Then the door opened and Mr. Cartwright stood in the doorway looking at her. His face looked flushed, as if he had been drinking, but there couldn't have been time for that.

"Yes?" he said shortly.

"Good evening, Mr. Cartwright," she said genially. "I just came to call on your wife. I told her I'd drop in again."

His look was utterly blank, as if he'd forgotten not only who she was, but all the amenities of a traveling tour group.

"May I come in?" Mrs. Wagstaff persisted pleasantly. A low, moaning sound started behind him in the cottage.

"What?" His face changed slowly . . . as if civilization were seeping back into it. "Yes. Yes, of course." He turned abruptly, moving away from the door. "Here's Mrs. Wagstaff, dear, come to see you."

His face as he looked at his wife was set in a rictus of . . . pain? Despair? Irritation? In that brick-colored complexion, it was hard to tell.

"She'll be glad to see you," he said, in a voice completely without gladness. "I'm going out for a walk. I'll see you later."

The door shut firmly behind his white-clad figure. He seemed always to wear white shirts and duck pants . . . except, Mrs. Wagstaff thought, when he wore a dark blue sweater. She glanced toward the chair, but it was empty tonight.

Mrs. Cartwright sat in her chair, her head trembling slightly on her thin neck. There was nothing to show any reason for her cry. Just her great, gray eyes staring, and a crease between her brows. That sound, Mrs. Wagstaff thought suddenly, was almost involuntary. Whatever she had to express could only come out with great effort, and would sound like some wild howl. She had heard it before, after all, when nothing untoward seemed to be happening. But it had seemed particularly loud, like on that day when Mrs. Cartwright sat beside the cenote and her husband's hands dropped away from the wheelchair.

"It must be a bore for you being in the house so much," she said, and was immediately disgusted to have used such stupid language. Boredom indeed! What a word to use for the catastrophe of this woman's life. She wanted to tell the professor to watch where Mr. Cartwright went, but she couldn't just walk out now. Instead, she pulled up a chair and sat down. On the theory that the invalid knew little of what was going on, she launched into a good, gossipy stream of talk about the tour people, the tragedy, the activities of the police. The trouble with invalids was that everyone was hypnotized by their physical problem and couldn't even talk to them in normal tones about everyday interests. Well, she would try.

While she talked, her eyes wandered about the room. It was very tidy tonight. The maid must have been in. Mrs. Cartwright's night-gown, open all the way down the back like a hospital gown, lay neatly waiting on the bed. There was water, and a bottle of pills on the bedstand, and a picture in a leather frame.

"Is that your daughter?" Mrs. Wagstaff asked. The gray eyes stayed open, but the frown deepened. She looked again at the picture. There was clearly a resemblance between the young woman in it and the poor creature in the wheelchair. "Oh," she said, "perhaps your sister?" The lids closed and lay there as if asleep for a long moment before they opened again. Her sister. Of course. She looked young enough to be a daughter, but it was the stroke which had aged Mrs. Cartwright. If that woman was her sister, she, Mrs. Cartwright, was probably not more than forty herself!

"She looks like you," said Mrs. Wagstaff. The gray eyes looked at the pictured face, and the fine lips grew soft.

"She has a good, warm face," Mrs. Wagstaff went on. The invalid stared at a large, straw bag in a corner of the room and her one movable hand scrabbled, pointing.

"Shall I get something for you from your bag?" The eyes said yes. Mrs. Wagstaff brought the bag and opened it before her. It had toilet articles and a few pieces of lingerie and an envelope of pictures. "These?" She held up the envelope. Yes. She drew them out. They were wedding pictures. And the bride was the sister. No! Not the sister. The bride was Mrs. Cartwright! There she stood in a garden in a pretty white silk dress and a broad-brimmed, flowered hat. Behind her was a golden forsythia bush, and beside her was Mr. Cartwright . . . looking very pink and broadly smiling . . . and not much younger than he did now.

Mrs. Wagstaff slipped the pictures through her fingers. There was a picture of a table outdoors and a cake and the wedding party holding champagne glasses. And Mrs. Cartwright, looking just like her sister, but far more radiant, held her husband's arm, or smiled at him, or handed him a piece of cake . . . all without a guess that the sky was to blacken so soon. When she looked up, there was a wet streak sliding down Mrs. Cartwright's cheek.

Mrs. Wagstaff went and put her big hand on Mrs. Cartwright's shoulder. "It *is* a cruel trick," she said, with a twitch of anger in her voice. Life played such *vile* games! Then, to shift the subject slightly, she said, "These pictures can't have been very long ago. Ten years?" The eyes stayed open. "Eight? Seven? Six?" And the eyes closed and opened again. Yes. Six years! And she had been stricken for three of them! How awful. How awful for them both. Awe-ful in the biblical sense. No wonder Mr. Cartwright looked bitter. Small wonder, for that matter, if he could be so hypnotized by Barbara. He probably wasn't more than forty-five. Mrs. Wagstaff looked at the pictures in her hand because she couldn't, for the moment, look at Mrs. Cartwright sitting pale and fragile and immobile in her chair. Nothing either of them could do would surprise her any more. If he had killed Barbara . . . if he wanted, even, to kill his wife, she could understand the impulse. How could one bear such a thing . . . for a lifetime?

She got up abruptly. "I'll put these away for you," she said. She set the chair back in its corner and looked around. "Is there something I can get for you? Something to eat? Or drink? Or will you come to dinner later with your husband? *Do* come. It's tedious to stay so much in your cottage. The group has its amusing sides to watch."

Mrs. Cartwright's lips stretched into a faint smile, and her eyelids drooped. Yes.

"Good. I'll see you at dinner then, when your husband gets back."

She pressed her shoulder again, gently, and went out. It was already quite dark, except for the rings of light on the path from the lamps.

Professor Michelson was sitting on a stone bench beside the pool.

"Ah," he said. "I thought you had been held for ransom."

"We were talking," she said. "Well, *I* was talking." She paused to let the sore feeling in her chest quiet down. It didn't do to get upset about *anything*. It just wasted one's resources.

"What was the matter with her?"

"Nothing I could see. Except, of course, everything. I guess she makes that sound when she wants to communicate, but I don't know what caused it this time. She's coming to dinner when her husband gets back. Did you see him? Where did he go?"

"Yes, I saw him. He went toward the front of the hotel, rather fast. I almost followed him, but I expected you'd be right out."

"Too bad," she said regretfully, "but I don't expect he was doing anything very damaging. It's too dark for searching . . . and the police have probably covered the whole area by now."

"Just a walk, I suppose . . . though the mind boggles at a murderer doing anything so ordinary. Well, are you coming to dinner?"

"Yes. As soon as I clean up a bit."

"I, too. It might be useful to keep an eye on them at dinner."

She nodded, and the professor bobbed off down the path, his bald head gleaming under each lamp.

But they didn't do a surveillance job at dinner. The Cartwrights didn't come to dinner.

DINNER WAS LATE . . . AND BOISTEROUS. THE MEMBERS of the tour group were busily telling the new tourists all about their horrible experience of the morning. Mrs. Gibson was complaining bitterly because the group was not allowed to go on.

"It had to be someone from this awful place that did it," she said. "Or maybe José!"

That figured, thought Mrs. Wagstaff. What Mrs. Gibson meant was that it had to be one of the "other" people, the *natives.* And of course, she might have been right. Except for the oddness of Mr. Cartwright's actions. But José had been acting rather odd too. Where *was* José, by the way? She looked about the crowded dining room. Everyone looked flushed and lively. The tiny, plump waitresses in their white huipils were almost running between the tables. But there was no José . . . and, she now observed, no Cartwrights. Perhaps Mrs. Cartwright had been unable to persuade her husband. She could imagine that with such an invalid, it would often seem simpler to him to have a tray sent to their cottage. She sighed and looked down at her beans. The refried beans were one of the few really great Mexican dishes . . . but she had no heart for them tonight.

"How long do we have to stay here?" asked Mrs. Bernardi anxiously. "I must be home soon."

"Fat chance," said Mrs. Gibson. "I know these people. Inefficiency is their middle name. We'll be here till the cows come home. What are they *doing*, anyway? They haven't even talked to us yet!"

"Well," said Mr. Gumbiner mildly, "it's only been one day. You can't expect miracles." "Well, *I've* had enough of this place," said Mrs. Gibson resoundingly. "We were supposed to go on to Uxmal tomorrow. I don't suppose that's in the cards now. Where on earth is José? He ought to be able to tell us! What are we paying him for anyhow?"

"I doubt that he knows any more than we do," said Mrs. Wagstaff. "It is all up to the police." Not that she had much more confidence in them than Mrs. Gibson. She, too, wondered where José was. She had not seen him, nor except for that one brief glimpse on the road, Señor Ruz, all day. Dinner was like a great, buzzing hive of bees. It was already ten after nine, and they had not yet had their dessert. She looked at the menu card. Creme caramel or ice cream. Again. It didn't do to count on dessert in Mexico or in China. France and Austria were the places for sweets . . . and of course, the U.S.A.

"I believe," said Mrs. Wagstaff, rising, and dropping her gunny sack off her lap, "I will forego dessert tonight. It has been a long day."

The professor picked up her diet tables and her mosquito spray and handed them up to her. "Shall I escort you?" he asked gallantly.

Mrs. Gibson's face was a sketch. The quirk on Mrs. Wagstaff's face deepened into a broad grin. "Thank you, Augustus," she said, "but it is not necessary. I shall see you in the morning. Good night all."

But it was not a good night. The garden was quiet enough, but when she got to her cottage she heard the noise of stifled sobbing from next door. It was like a battle trumpet, and without hesitation, she knocked and went in.

Susan was lying across her bed, her face a ruin of tears. Or as much a ruin as a twenty-year-old face can be, thought Mrs. Wagstaff.

She took her own advice. Without a word, she sat down on the bed and took the girl into her large, padded arms. Slowly the sobs turned to hiccups, and Susan's hand came up to swab her eyes.

"What is it?" Mrs. Wagstaff offered a Kleenex.

"Oh, everything is pure *hell!*" the girl said. She pushed away, not looking at Mrs. Wagstaff.

"It *hasn't* been a good day," Mrs. Wagstaff conceded. "But what in *particular* is it just now?" The theory was that everyone in trouble needed to talk . . . no matter about what, or to whom. Mrs. Wagstaff had read the books.

"Well . . ." she paused, hiccuping, as if she didn't want to say any more, but Mrs. Wagstaff was a presence not to be denied. "Well . . . my uncle is just about speechless. I did what you said. I hugged him. And you know, it did seem to help. But of course, it didn't *last.* We had a sort of dinner up there, but Uncle Larry hardly said boo . . . and Brian was even worse. He looked so far away . . . oh, I don't know." She looked at Mrs. Wagstaff with eyes dark with more grief. What *was* it, Mrs. Wagstaff wondered. Loss? Anger?

"I thought that *now,* he'd . . ." Susan stopped abruptly. "Well, when I went into the artifacts tent after dinner, he yelled at me as if I were a . . . a workman! And he'd showed me everything just yesterday. He said I wasn't to touch anything!"

"And *did* you?" Mrs. Wagstaff asked.

But Susan, from the bowels of her own misery, pursued her own thoughts, "I think he must *hate* me . . . you know, because I'm alive, and she's not!"

"Well, you mustn't be surprised at that," said Mrs. Wagstaff. "After all, if he was in love with her, he *would* be pretty upset. Were they . . . engaged?"

"I don't know for sure. Barbara *informed* me that he was private territory. But I know it wasn't anything official." The sarcasm of that "informed" seemed to strike her, for she made a face.

"Where is he now?"

"I don't know. He brought me back after dinner—they have an early dinner at the dig—and then he went away. I haven't seen him since around eight. I guess he's gone back. And I don't know what to do. I'm no use to *anyone* here. Do you think we can soon go home?"

"I don't know. It will be up to the police how long we have to stay." She repeated Mr. Gumbiner's words, "It's only been one day."

She patted the girl gently. "If you want to be a help, you might see what you can do for Mrs. Cartwright tomorrow. She needs people to talk to her, I think. And right now, the best thing to do is to get into bed with a good book and go to sleep early. Wait. I have just the thing." She dredged into the depths of her sack and brought out Isabella Bird's *A Lady's Life in the Rocky Mountains*. It was her theory that when one really wanted taking out of oneself, the best thing to read was not light fiction but somebody else's life. Other people . . . other *real* people, that is . . . had such absorbing trials that one lost one's own isolated misery in contemplating theirs. Even mysteries, which she loved, were not the thing when the world was literally too much with us. The book had, at least, the immediate effect of bringing a smile to Susan's lips. Even if it was slightly satirical.

"Thanks. I'll try it," said Susan. Mrs. Wagstaff could almost see the words in Susan's head . . . she's a nice old thing! An awful thought! Was she indeed so bland?

Her own side of the cottage looked bland enough, strewn with books on the Maya, mysteries, and Jane Austen, whom she took everywhere to read when she had a cold and felt wretched. Certain books were simply *healing,* whatever their literary virtues or vices. *Pride and Prejudice* had always cleared her up better than Dristan.

She took off her corset gratefully and looked down. No question about it. She did rather . . . billow . . . without it. But who cared? When she had performed her ablutions and gotten into bed, she was prepared to read for an hour or two . . . but it *had* been a long day. She was asleep in twenty minutes, her bed lamp still lit.

She was asleep, and she was dreaming that she was in the arctic wilderness. There were nothing but broken snowfields as far as she could see. But there were wolves. From a group of moving black dots on the horizon came a terrifying howling. And they were coming towards her . . . fast. The wild, lonely sound of their howls was paralyzing. She stood rigid and unmoving till the pack was upon her, the great moaning howls almost at her throat. Then with a smothered shriek, she sat upright in bed, her eyes dilated with horror. The room was flat and still under the lamplight, but the howl seemed to pursue her from dream to waking. Her traveling clock on the bed said two o'clock. She sat for a moment trying to collect her thoughts. The cry came again, and she knew she was awake. She was out of bed in a moment and throwing on her blue flannel robe. She knew that sound. Her feet thrust into her slippers, she went out onto the cottage porch. Susan's light was out. The garden was bathed in moonlight, but the shadows were black under the shrubberies. There was no sound now, but she went down the path, skirted the swimming pool, and approached the Cartwrights' cottage without hesitating. The light was on inside, and through the unshaded window she could see Mrs. Cartwright sitting in her chair. Beside her on the unwrinkled bed lay her nightgown. There was no one else in the cottage.

When she went in, Mrs. Cartwright's huge gray eyes glared at her like those of a madwoman. And then, as though exhausted, they slid closed and her head sagged back against her chair.

"Mrs. Cartwright! Are you alone? Are you all right?" The eyes didn't open. Mrs. Wagstaff glanced into the empty bathroom, and looked about the room. There was no change from the afternoon. The nightgown still lay there. The room was completely tidy. There was no sign of a dinner tray.

"Where is your husband?" she asked. "Didn't he come back after I left you?"

The gray eyes opened and looked at her with a great weariness.

"Have you been sitting here alone all this time?" Mrs. Wagstaff's voice shook with anger. "Come, I'll help you to bed." The eyes stared at her and then at the room. There was not just weariness in them now. There was apprehension. They moved about the room, stopping at the closet and the window, then circling again, and back to the window.

"Let me get you to bed," said Mrs. Wagstaff, "and then I'll see where your husband has gone." If it had been a couple of nights ago, she thought savagely, he would probably have been prowling about after Barbara. Where he was tonight, God only knew. He might have had all he could stand. He might have fled, leaving his wife, leaving a murder investigation he feared, fleeing into the night.

She lifted Mrs. Cartwright out of the chair. Even as dead, unhelpful weight, she wasn't much of a burden. She drew her clothes off, took her to the bathroom, put the poor, wasted body into the nightgown, and lowered her gently onto the bed. Her cheeks looked sunken with exhaustion, and, almost at once, she was asleep.

Mrs. Wagstaff stood a moment, considering. If Mr. Cartwright had really skipped, he must have done so hours ago. What was she to do? She didn't like to leave Mrs. Cartwright alone like this. Someone should stay with her. With a nod of decision, she went out of the cottage and down the walk to the next cottage. This was a double with the professor on one side and Mrs. Gibson on the other. She would get them both. She tapped firmly on Professor Michelson's door.

The professor was a heavy sleeper . . . but Mrs. Gibson wasn't. She came to her door and peered out.

"Who is it?" she demanded suspiciously. Then she recognized Mrs. Wagstaff. Her eyes widened with shock . . . and then, almost at once, with vindicated pleasure. Mrs. Wagstaff! In her bathrobe! Knocking at the professor's door in the middle of the night! It was almost too good to be true!

But her triumph didn't last long. Just long enough to amuse Mrs. Wagstaff by its transparency.

"Mrs. Gibson, would you go over and stay with Mrs. Cartwright, please?" she said. "Something is wrong. Mr. Cartwright hasn't come back and she's been left alone. I've gotten her to bed, but I think she shouldn't be alone."

"Oh." The tone was clearly disappointed. "Why, where did he go?"

"I don't know that," said Mrs. Wagstaff patiently. "I was going to get Professor Michelson to investigate."

"Oh," said Mrs. Gibson again. "Well, yes, sure. I'll just get something on. Shouldn't you call the police?"

"Possibly." Mrs. Wagstaff looked at her thoughtfully. "Of course he may just have gone out moongazing."

"Huh!" Mrs. Gibson knew better than *that.*

But the professor was up now. His light blinked on and he came to the door to see what all the fuss was about at this ungodly hour. He was in his pajamas, bright green pajamas with a dragon on the front of them. Above the dragon's fire-breathing mouth his white beard bubbled in sleepy disarray.

"What is it?" he asked. "What has happened? Elaine?"

"Yes. We need you, Augustus." She outlined the problem once again. He let out a soft whistle and rubbed his hand back and forth over his bald head.

"I think you should tell the lieutenant," said Mrs. Gibson.

"Well, now, why don't I take a look around, first. Maybe he's right around here. Perhaps he has had a fall, or a heart attack."

"Maybe he's in someone else's cottage," said Mrs. Gibson acidly.

"Well, if he is, there is nothing we can do about it. I don't propose to knock on everyone's door to find out," said the professor.

"I suggest we take that look around," said Mrs. Wagstaff. "If you will stay with Mrs. Cartwright, Mrs. Gibson, I'll dress and be back in a few minutes."

"All right," said Mrs. Gibson without enthusiasm.

The colloquy over, the three went their ways in the moonlight. Apparently they had waked no one else. Someone was supposed to have been left on guard overnight, but there was utter silence now in the garden. It was 3 A.M.

THE HOME-STYLE VIGILANTE COMMITTEE WAS UN-
successful. Mrs. Wagstaff, dressed, met the professor, in pants
and a shirt, beside the swimming pool. He was shivering in the
predawn chill, but his eyes were shining with interest. "I have had
no luck," he said, "but I've only explored three paths. Would you
take that end of the garden, Elaine?"

"Yes. I'll look in on the main building too." She peered at him
a moment. His teeth chattered faintly. "I would suggest, professor,
that you put on a sweater first."

"Quite right. It's enough to freeze the ba . . . to freeze the blood."

"Or the balls off a brass monkey," she agreed calmly. His head
cocked, startled. *Another man who thinks we live on clouds and
drink only nectar*, she grinned to herself invisibly. *Only Gerald had
known her complete vocabulary . . . and he didn't always approve.*

They parted. She marched down one path after another, bending,
with a creak of corsets, to look in the shadows of the trees. She
wasn't sure why she was doing that. Mr. Cartwright didn't seem the
type to pass out drunkenly under a bush. On the other hand, he *did*

seem choleric enough to have had a heart attack . . . in which case he might be lying anywhere. But he wasn't in the garden. She looked thoughtfully at the garden gate. A policeman, they had been told, would be on duty there all night. But there was no one. The sky was paling as she entered the hotel from the terrace door. One dim light burned over the desk, but there was no one about here either. It wasn't the Hilton. It didn't occur to anyone here in Yucatán that in a hotel there should always be someone awake. Or perhaps the switchboard had been switched over to the manager's room for possible night calls. It didn't matter, except that she was always interested in the running of things. Anyway, there was no one in the lounge. The bottles behind the bar glimmered in the dawn light from the terrace doors. The dining room was silent and empty. She glanced down the two bedroom corridors, but there was no sign of anyone, and, like the professor, she had no intention of seeking Mr. Cartwright out of anyone's bed. She didn't know where the manager's room was, nor whether Lieutenant Molo was here or back in the village for the night.

At last she wandered out to the front steps and looked through the trees toward the road. The moon was just sinking, and birds had begun to twitter. But of human presence there was none.

Then the professor came around the corner of the building, muffled in a great, woolly red sweater.

"I see you have not found him," he said.

"No," she said. "Has it occurred to you that he may be *escaping*? Perhaps we *should* go to the police."

They contemplated that idea without enthusiasm.

"But," she went on, "I don't know where to find the lieutenant. Perhaps, since it's so near dawn, we might as well wait a bit till someone is up and we can ask where to find him. I don't like to knock indiscriminately."

He looked at the garden gate. "Remarkable inefficiency that there should be no one on duty," he said. "Or perhaps"—he wanted to be fair—"someone was left on duty and has fallen asleep somewhere."

They stood silently, listening to the birds. "The trouble is," he went on finally, "that once awake, I am through with sleep for this night."

"Gerald was like that. I had to be very careful not to wake him. I myself can sleep at any hour. Or wake, too." She looked up at the sky. "Right now, however, I am awake . . . and it is not too far from my morning walk time. Would you care to walk a little?"

"I shall certainly not let you walk alone," said the professor firmly.

They walked out toward the road. Marched would have been a better word. Mrs. Wagstaff tended to march when she was in form . . . and she had been sightseeing for weeks now. Professor Michelson, engulfed in his red sweater, trotted beside her like a terrier beside a mastiff.

They turned automatically toward the pyramid field. In the other direction there was nothing but hemp fields and occasional huts.

"It is not a place *I* would have chosen to build a city," said the professor.

"Nor I. I expect they were pushed here from some more attractive and better watered areas."

"Better watered! There is *no* water here. How incredible to conceive of building a city where there was no water supply!"

"Don't forget the cenote."

They looked at each other, suddenly remembering the cenote.

"I should not care to drink out of *that*," said the professor gravely.

They walked around the base of Kukulcan. The stillness of the great stone monster was like a weight on them. Quietly, without looking back at it, they walked across the field in the wan light. Birds were chirping madly now from all the columns of the temple of the warriors.

"*Listen* to them," said the professor. They paused. There seemed to be birds sitting on the top of every pillar, some kind of blackbird.

"There are *white* birds in the Chac Mool," said Mrs. Wagstaff, peering ahead at the strange, reclining stone figure before the temple.

"Yes. I guess they . . ." He stopped dead still, staring. "Oh, God," he said.

"What?"

"Elaine. You wait here a minute. I'll be right back. I want to see something." He started toward the temple, but she was by his side.

"What is it, Augustus," she demanded in her deepest voice.

"Elaine . . . those are not birds. I think we've found Cartwright."

Together they approached the Chac Mool. It lay there, the statue of a man in stone, reclining on its back. Lying on top of it, on *his* back, his loosened white shirt fluttering slightly in the early breeze, was Mr. Cartwright. His head hung backwards over the end of the Chac Mool, and his chest was covered with blood.

THE SOUND OF THE BIRDS WAS LIKE AN OCEAN ROAR IN her ears as she looked. Beside her the professor was making a curious, swallowing sound, but she couldn't turn her eyes away to look at him. Mr. Cartwright, newly dead, drew her eyes like a magnet. It took several minutes of paralysis before she realized that he was not newly dead. The massive gout of blood all over his chest was already clotted. His face, in life brick-red, was as white as though there were no blood left in him, white except for two odd streaks of blue on his cheeks. She drew in a deep breath and held it, held it till her heart began to thump and her face felt queer and numb.

The professor's voice seem to come from a long way away. "We must get the police."

They went, then, half running, stumbling, back across the field to the road. For Mrs. Wagstaff, the run, her heart thumping in her chest, was like a ghastly rerun of a horror film, How could this be happening to her a second time?

She stopped suddenly, near the gate, and looked back.

"Should we leave him alone?"

"Alone: Good God, woman, he's *dead!* There's a madman loose in this place. Come *on.*" He seized her hand and half dragged her onto the road.

The light had that luminous glow it gets just before the sun thrusts up over the treetops, and the birds were everywhere. They were almost back to the hotel before they saw anything that lived. And that was a sleepy-looking woman scratching herself in the dusty yard of her hut. She stared at them with impassive wonder as they went by.

One of the maids, a tiny creature with her huipil tucked up, was washing the tile floor when they staggered into the hotel lobby.

"Where is the lieutenant?" Professor Michelson demanded.

The girl looked surprised. Just that. Nothing more.

"We must find the policeman. Police. Do you understand?"

She clearly didn't. By now Mrs. Wagstaff had gotten her breath back.

"Polizia," she said firmly. "Donde esta Señor Molo?"

"O." Instantly the little creature burst into a torrent of Spanish.

"Oh, lord," said the professor, his furry eyebrows working, "what is she saying?"

"I don't know," said Mrs. Wagstaff. "That's the great language problem. I've learned enough to ask the questions ... but not enough to understand the answers. Certainly not at this speed." She stopped the girl by grasping her tiny arm. "Donde? Montrez-moi."

The girl looked puzzled by the sudden intrusion of French, but something must have penetrated, for she nodded several times and led the way down one of the corridors. Her knock produced a question, and suddenly the door opened and Lieutenant Molo looked at them. He was in uniform, as if he had been up all night.

"What is it?" he said, after one glance at their faces.

"Mr. Cartwright," said Mrs. Wagstaff. "He's dead."

"Dead?"

"Yes. Dead. Murdered. He's in the field."

He stared at them for a moment, his brown face almost ludicrously startled. "Dead?" Finally his eyes narrowed and a look of guile came into them. "How did you happen to find him?" he asked.

"What is the difference? We were out for a walk. Come *on.*"

Lieutenant Molo glanced at his watch. It was half past five.

"Are you coming?" asked the professor impatiently. His beard seemed to have lost its aggressive curl, and hung, damp with sweat. "Elaine, perhaps you had better stay here."

She was about to protest when she suddenly thought about Mrs. Cartwright. "Yes," she said heavily. "I'll stay."

She went out into the garden. The sun had just come up and bushes were steaming in the new warmth. It seemed hours since they had roamed about in the half-light, looking for Mr. Cartwright, somewhat reluctant to follow up their brilliant hypothesis about him, not quite ready to get the police, to make a fuss.

Her stomach rumbled. No doubt about it. She felt decidedly queer. Partly it was that horror in the field. But partly it was the unexpectedness of it. She had been so *sure,* in her own mind, that Mr. Cartwright had killed Barbara that it made no sense for *him* to be murdered. It was as if all her logical props had been knocked out from under her. If he was really a victim, then someone else had to be a murderer, and all her clever conclusions about sweaters and jealousy and lust and wanting to kill his wife . . . all of that had to mean something else. Or nothing.

She looked into the Cartwrights' window before starting to knock. She could just see the top of Mrs. Cartwright's head on the pillow. Mrs. Gibson, a shocking-pink sweater draped over her arms, was asleep in the chair. Nothing stirred.

She decided what she needed was to go back to her own cottage for a few minutes to wash her face. Washing her face, she had always found, was helpful when you were disorganized. But it wasn't that easy. The gardeners were out now, and her little boy of the tortilla was all ready for her. With a brilliant, toothless smile—he had lost all four front teeth—he threw his ball at her. Almost as a reflex, she caught it and sent it back. Then, of course, she had to play at least for a few minutes. Throwing only *one* ball was like trying to eat one peanut. Impossible. When she finally got back to her cottage and washed her face, the sun was well up.

It was there that Professor Michelson found her when he came back. His face, when she came to answer his knock, was so white that she was alarmed.

"Come in, Augustus," she said, and half pushed him into a chair. He sat gratefully.

"He sent me back to get his sergeant. He said to stay put. Elaine . . . ?"

"Yes. What is it?"

The words seemed to coagulate in his throat, tangled in the bush of his beard. "Elaine," he said, starting over.

"Yes?"

"He wasn't . . . just shot."

"You mean he was knifed?"

"Not just that."

She stared at him. "What happened to him then? Augustus? *Professor!*"

"His heart had been cut out!"

"What?"

"It was in a bowl . . . on the ground beside him!"

TIME WAS, WHEN THE WORLD WAS YOUNG AND MORE OR less innocent, when the biggest journalistic draw was supposed to be anything about Lincoln's doctor's dog. Nowadays, thought Mrs. Wagstaff wryly, it has to be a case of violence, preferably brutal, performed with a sharp-edged tool, and set, if at all possible, in a distant and romantic background. On all those counts, the murder of Harvey Cartwright qualified. The peace of Chichén Itzá was shattered with an influx of reporters from Mexico City and an AP man who flew in from New Orleans. They grabbed hold of anyone conceivably connected with the murders and they dragged their cameras all over the field and down to the cenote. They even persuaded one of the hotel waiters—at a price—to pose for them in the exact position of Cartwright's body. Within twenty-four hours the place had been transformed. Lieutenant Molo, looking grim and harassed, was on his metal—trying to do everything, and to forestall the sending down of an inspector from Mexico City. Everyone on the tour had now been interrogated—twice—but no one knew with what results.

"I *told* him I'd gone to bed early," said Mrs. Gibson crossly, "but he sure didn't look as if he believed me!" She glared across the luncheon table at Mrs. Wagstaff. "If you go on any *more* morning walks, God knows who you'll find next!"

Mrs. Crummit let out a wan little squeak. She wasn't alone. The circumstances of Cartwright's death had shocked them all. It was one thing for a man to be shot by gangsters. It was quite another for him to be found with his heart cut out and left neatly beside him.

"It's a maniac," said one of the blue-haired ladies, her voice trembling. "Someone is imitating those horrible sacrifices! I think we should be let go home. It's *dangerous* here!"

"Fat chance," said Mrs. Gibson. "*I* think we should call the American ambassador and make him get us out of here. Any one of us could be next!"

Mrs. Wagstaff couldn't deny it. Not only had Mr. Cartwright's heart been cut out, but from the raggedness of the wound, it had evidently been done with some rather crude weapon—like an ancient obsidian knife. No weapon had been found. The bowl was of a pottery native to the area, and too common to trace.

Then there was the strange blue on Mr. Cartwright's face. Blue was the color of sacrifice. Victims were often painted blue before they were killed. Mrs. Wagstaff had read Bishop Landa on the subject. Not that she had any intention of bringing this up. Susan looked cobalt enough herself without any outside help. She sat stiffly at the table, her hair tied back tightly, her eyes wide and unfocused.

"How come you're not up with your uncle?" Mrs. Gibson asked her all at once. She started.

"Oh. He says . . . I mean he thinks . . . I should be here. He says it's more comfortable . . . and safer."

"*Safer!* Huh! They're all *alive* up there. It's our tour that seems to be getting wiped out!"

"I don't know," the girl said, her brows drawn into a frown. "I asked to stay with him, but he said . . . and Brian said . . ." Her eyes suddenly fixed.

Mrs. Wagstaff, looking over her shoulder, saw that José had come in. He looked odd, that peculiar grayish color that dark-skinned people sometimes get when they are ill. Or upset. His great brown eyes seemed to have no whites to them. He came directly to their table.

"Ladies," he said. "The police have told your bus driver that he can return to Mérida."

"Our *bus* driver! What about *us*? I've had enough of this place to last me the rest of my life!" Mrs. Gibson was furious. "If he goes we're stranded here!"

"No. Please do not distress yourself," José said. "He can be recalled as soon as we are allowed to leave."

"And when will that be?" asked Mrs. Wagstaff.

José shrugged. "They do not tell me that."

In fact, despite all the feverish activity about the hotel, remarkably little information seemed to be forthcoming. Everyone asked everyone else what had been said in the interviews with the lieutenant, but either nothing significant had come out . . . or someone wasn't going to tell. José, as an official of the tour, made a half-hearted attempt to organize some sightseeing for the afternoon, but nobody took him up on it. There was, in fact, a marked withdrawal from José and from everyone else of native extraction.

"It's pretty clear," said Mrs. Gibson ominously, "that whoever did it is two things: a maniac, and someone who knows all about native rituals!" She stared hard at José's retreating back, and then switched her gaze to Mrs. Wagstaff. "You know more about them than any of us," she said . . . and paused.

"Yes." Mrs. Wagstaff nodded. "And I have, on occasion, been considered a bit . . . peculiar. I should advise you not to get me upset, Mrs. Gibson." Mrs. Gibson stared at her, her jowls quivering. Mrs. Wagstaff rose majestically and put down her napkin. "If you will excuse me?" The table full of people looked after her dumbly, but she was not leaving from pique. She had seen the little sergeant on Molo's staff beckon to José, and her curiosity bump had grown no smaller.

She went out onto the terrace and glanced casually at the door to the lounge that the lieutenant had taken over as an office. The

French door was open a crack, and she leaned against the wall beside it.

"You are related." Molo's voice was stating, not questioning.

"Yes." José volunteered nothing.

"You know then if he writes English?"

A pause. "Yes, of course."

Molo didn't sound surprised. "Now, where was he last night?"

She did not, she was sure, *imagine* the tremor in José's voice, like a man uncertain what to say next. "I . . . don't know."

She straightened suddenly. Señor Ruz was approaching through the garden.

Smoothly—Mrs. Wagstaff didn't believe in making excuses for her actions—she walked toward him.

"I've been trying to hear what is going on," she told him frankly. "We are all very worried, and no one will tell us anything. Do you know what is happening?"

His eyes on her face were as sharp as needles. "I am called," he said, and then, venom escaping from him like an uncontrollable steam, he went past her along the terrace, paused for a moment outside the terrace door, rapped harshly, and went in.

She looked after him thoughtfully. A strange man. It seemed she had never seen him other than angry. She could understand that he might resent the suddenly universal suspicion toward all the natives. But he had been angry before. He had been angry the night she had seen him and José at the pool. What was it he had said? Something about remembering who he, José, *was*. Well, who *was* he? As far as they knew, he was just a rather attractive travel guide. Evidently he was something more, at least to Señor Ruz. Just what *was* the connection between the two men?

She started down the path toward the Cartwright cottage. Mrs. Bernardi had been left to cope long enough. Yesterday, after Mrs. Wagstaff had broken the news to Mrs. Cartwright that her husband was dead—she had had to say murdered, but she had *not* had to say *how*—she had gathered the other ladies and asked everyone to take turns day and night staying with Mrs. Cartwright until other arrangements could be made. Nervous and uncomfortable as the job made them, they had had the grace not to demur.

Now approaching the little cottage for her turn, she thought about Mrs. Cartwright's face. It was an interesting face. The paralysis had drawn her lip down a little on one side, but her face was still capable of expression. And her expression, when Mrs. Wagstaff had told her, had been unexpected. There was shock in the downward dart of the fine eyebrows, but almost at once, there was something else. It wasn't easy to put a name to so fleeting a thing, but Mrs. Wagstaff had no doubt in her own mind. Mrs. Cartwright was relieved. Not happy. But relieved . . . as if some great burden were off her. Whatever her reasons, she had been no trouble to take care of. She had not gone off into a bellowing session. In fact, quite the contrary, she had been utterly silent, her gray, listening eyes as still as pools.

How queer everyone was, Mrs. Wagstaff thought. "We're all mad except thee and me, and sometimes I think thee's a bit mad too." It was a cliché that had always amused Gerald. They had . . . like most happy couples . . . always thought of themselves as an enclave of sanity in a mad world, although of course they had never said so to anyone else. Gerald, a historian, had a perfect vantage point for noticing insanity. *She* had always been curious about people . . . and that, certainly, was another kind of vantage point for making the same observation.

Well, Mrs. Cartwright was relieved. Why not? If her husband was not the murderer, he might still have been a disaster as a husband. A disaster . . . perhaps even dangerous. She remembered his choleric face, and those powerful hands lifting, fractionally, from the handles of the wheelchair. All right. Nothing insane, then, about Mrs. Cartwright's reaction.

Señor Ruz was a horse of another color. Why was he perpetually angry? Why did he so clearly despise the tourists? He had been little short of rude to everyone . . . utterly hopeless as a ruins guide, though he seemed to know all about them.

A man in uniform stood near the cottage. He stiffened at her approach, but said nothing.

As she went up onto the little cottage porch, the door opened and one of the tiny maids came out with a tray. She was evidently clearing away Mrs. Cartwright's and Mrs. Bernardi's lunch.

"Ah," said Mrs. Wagstaff, and delayed the girl with a light touch on the arm. "Hable usted Ingles?"

The girl, a bright little robin of plump brown, smiled widely.

"Si, si, good Ingles, Señora."

"Good," said Mrs. Wagstaff. "I wanted to ask you if you have seen Señor Ruz. The lieutenant wants him."

"Oh, si. Yes. No, I have not see. I make beds. I look?"

"No, never mind. Perhaps he has been found by José. José has been looking for him. He will probably know where to find him. They are . . . friends, yes?"

The little maid's smile was ravishing. She was having the rare opportunity of a conversation in English. With good English, she might get a job better than this fetching and carrying. She might become a hotel clerk or a shopgirl in an establishment for tourists. "Oh, yes. José know. Señor Ruz is mother's brother . . . aunt?"

"Uncle. Yes, of course. Thank you very much." Nodding and smiling, Mrs. Wagstaff went on into the cottage. Lies were very useful. Obviously the world could not get along without them. All children should be taught efficient lying from birth. She had a new, small trifle of information, and there was no time now to do anything but file it away in her head, but it was interesting. Really quite interesting.

"Oh, there you are!" Mrs. Bernardi's tone was rapturously welcoming. She came to the door, her round face beaming. "I'm so glad you've come," she said, lowering her voice slightly. "Not that I mind staying with the poor thing, but she keeps . . . staring so, and I don't know whether to talk to her or not. The lieutenant sent word that he is coming to see her soon. Though I can't see what he can find out from her! Well . . . I'll leave you with her . . . is that all right?"

"Yes, certainly." Mrs. Wagstaff went into the dim recesses of the cottage. After the brilliant sun outside, it took a moment to see, but when she did, it looked as though nothing had changed in twenty-four hours. Mrs. Cartwright was sitting in her wheelchair, her head leaning against the back, her gray eyes looking straight ahead.

"Are you all right?" Mrs. Wagstaff asked.

The gray eyes closed and opened again.

"I don't know if they've told you that the policeman investigating will soon be here."

The eyes closed and opened again. Yes, she knew that.

"I don't know what I can tell you," Mrs. Wagstaff said frankly. "The police are all about, and have talked to everyone, but we don't know what they are doing." She didn't know whether Mrs. Cartwright had been told the details of her husband's death. She didn't believe in treating her like a cretin. On the other hand, the details were really too much to pass on to this speechless woman. The gray eyes drew down, and a line grew between the brows. She turned her head slightly toward the straw bag on the floor.

"Shall I get you something from your bag?" Yes. Mrs. Wagstaff picked up the bag and began to take things out of it. There were the wedding pictures again. And a small book. An address book. "This?" asked Mrs. Wagstaff. Yes. The address book. She opened it and looked at the names written in a fine, slanting, feminine hand. Mrs. Cartwright's clawed fingers scratched helplessly at the arm of her chair. They didn't look as though they could ever have written anything.

"Oh, yes," said Mrs. Wagstaff. How stupid of them all not to know. She wanted someone notified, someone called. She was utterly helpless here. "I'll read the names," she said. "You let me know when I get to the right one." She read through the pages, looking up after each name. "Anne Markham," she said at last, and the gray eyes closed wearily, relieved. "Is it your sister?" Mrs. Wagstaff asked gently. Yes. "I'll wire her at once!"

The knock on the door sounded thunderous in the gloom.

"Mrs. Cartwright?" Lieutenant Molo and his sergeant came into the room. He looked at Mrs. Wagstaff with a dismissing air.

"Shall I stay and help you talk to her?" Mrs. Wagstaff said grandly. "We have worked out a system." It was a system anybody could have worked out in ten seconds, but she hoped he wouldn't notice that. She wanted to stay. Mrs. Cartwright looked tense.

"Mmmnn-nn." The lieutenant was noncommittal.

"She has just asked me to send for her sister. I'll do that as soon as I've finished interpreting." There. Interpreting sounded very official. Molo tilted his great beak at her, looked helplessly at the invalid, and nodded.

"Will you ask her," he said in his gutteral voice, "exactly what time she saw her husband last?"

"You needn't ask *me*," said Mrs. Wagstaff. "She hears perfectly well. I will try to get her answer." She knew the answer, but she went through her interpretive rite anyway. "Four o'clock? Five? Six? Seven? Eight? Eight-thirty?" That was about the time she had come to call and Mr. Cartwright had gone out.

"Did he come back at all after that?" No.

"Do you know where he was going?"

Mrs. Cartwright frowned. She seemed to be straining to speak, but nothing came.

"He just said a walk," said Mrs. Wagstaff. "I was here."

Lieutenant Molo looked at her sharply. "You are everywhere, Mrs. Wagstaff."

"Not quite, unfortunately," she said calmly. "But I *was* calling on Mrs. Cartwright at the time Mr. Cartwright went out. He just said he was going for a walk."

The lieutenant stared out of the window a moment, and then gave a cough. "Mrs. Cartwright," he said, "I don't wish to offend, but had your husband made any . . . enemies on this trip? Had he, perhaps, had an unpleasantness with any member of the tour . . . or with any of the Yucatecs. The guides perhaps?"

No.

Mrs. Wagstaff recalled Mr. Cartwright's face when Barbara had favored Bothwell or José. But that could hardly forecast *this* murder. It would only make sense if one of *them* had been killed. Besides, the two murders could not be separated like this. They *had* to be related . . . and Barbara had been killed first. It seemed to Mrs. Wagstaff that the lieutenant was ignoring the most obvious line of questioning. Not so much *why* was Mr. Cartwright murdered . . . as why was he murdered in that particular *way*? Barbara thrown in the pool could, conceivably, have been merely convenient to the murderer, rather than ritualistic. Cartwright's murder could in no way have been *convenient*. It was, it had to be, conceived as a copy of a sacrificial rite. And if it was, then Barbara's death should be similarly considered. She suddenly remembered that odd smell near the cenote temple. Copal?

But the lieutenant was pursuing his own line. "Was he friendly with José Toron?" The eyes hesitated and then closed. Yes.

"There was no friction?" Molo persisted.

The gray eyes shivered fractionally, but did not close. No.

The police always asked the wrong questions, thought Mrs. Wagstaff, and so they got the wrong answers. Answers almost always need to be qualified. Unfortunately, Mrs. Cartwright's answers were limited to yeses and nos. Actually, she, Mrs. Wagstaff, had been present once when Mr. Cartwright had spoken quite nastily to José. But if anyone asked her if the two men were friendly, she would have to say yes, if the only alternative were no. One could hardly say that the two men were enemies. Neither yes nor no was adequate to explain. Mrs. Cartwright evidently thought so too. Her brows furrowed, but there was no way for her to expand her yeses and nos.

'The lieutenant stared at her for another moment, and shifted his feet uneasily. "Well . . . is there something we can do for you, Mrs. Cartwright? We have wired to your home."

The gray eyes shifted to Mrs. Wagstaff. Anxiously.

"I believe there is no one at her home to receive a wire," said Mrs. Wagstaff. "I will wire her sister immediately. I have her address here." She held up the address book. Lieutenant Molo nodded, relieved. The problem of Mrs. Cartwright was clearly a peculiarly difficult one for the local constabulary.

"In the meantime, I will see that the cottage is . . . protected."

"Protected?"

He nodded, shot a swift glance at Mrs. Cartwright, and turned to leave.

Protected. Mrs. Cartwright's thin face turned up to her, suddenly drawn and questioning. Protected?

"It's all right," said Mrs. Wagstaff, her large hand on the bony shoulders. "Until they know who killed your husband, they will keep watch over us all. That is only good sense."

Not, she thought, that the presence of the police had been of much use in saving Mr. Cartwright. Police surveillance was such a partial gesture! They clearly didn't have enough men. But there could *never* be enough. It is always easy to kill someone if one really wants to and is not afraid of the consequences. Police had never been able to save even so eminent a personage as a president. Of course, that is only true when the assassin doesn't care about saving himself. Like a kamikaze pilot, such a man is unstoppable. But who knew what kind of man was doing the killing here?

If there were any *reason* for these murders, then the killer was probably trying to protect himself. He might be cautious . . . deceptive. But if, as seemed likely, he was a madman, then perhaps he didn't care what happened to him . . . or didn't recognize the odds against him. In that case, he was probably impossible to stop . . . unless he could be caught in the act. It was a thought that lacked appeal.

She looked down suddenly. Her hand was still on Mrs. Cartwright's shoulder, and the shoulder was rigid; it almost seemed to exert a pressure upward into her hand.

"What is it?" she asked. The furrow between the brows was anguished. Mrs. Cartwright's hand scrabbled against the chair, a finger seemed to point. Down. Down at the floor. Toward the door.

"Something about the door? You want it locked?" No. "Opened?" No.

She went closer to the door and looked down. There was nothing to be seen . . . just the beautiful red tiles and some bits of grass from the feet of the policemen. When she looked back, Mrs. Cartwright was staring at her watch and then at the door with a sort of frenzied alternation.

"Something about the time." Mrs. Wagstaff pondered, her great chin sunk on her broad chest. "All right. I'll name times and you tell me if I've hit it." She glanced at her watch. "Three?" No. "Four?" No. "Five? Six? Seven?" Yes. "Is something going to happen at seven?" No. She looked at her scuffed brown shoes and considered. "Ah? *Did* something happen at seven? *Last night* at seven?" Ah! Mrs. Cartwright's eyes closed wearily. Yes.

Intuition struck Mrs. Wagstaff like light bulbs going on in her head. "Did someone come last night at seven to see your husband?"

The gray eyes stayed open, but the furrow was back. A moan of frustration broke from her lips and she looked once more at the floor near the door.

Thank God for charades, Mrs. Wagstaff thought. She liked games, and she was a whiz at charades. "Okay," she said. "so nobody came, but something happened that was connected to the door . . . or the floor beside the door. Yes?" Ah. Yes.

"Someone brought a message?"

Mrs. Cartwright shivered suddenly, but her eyes closed sharply and opened again.

"I see." Or so she said. She, herself, had stopped in last night shortly after seven, but there had been nothing to see then. Well, then, suppose someone had pushed a message under the door shortly before she had come. Suppose it was a message for Mr. Cartwright. Mrs. Cartwright would have seen him get it, but it was far too complicated for her to explain to the lieutenant.

"Do you know what was in the message?"

No.

"Was it shortly before I came?" Yes. So that message might have been what led him to his death. And Señor Ruz could write English!

"Do you know what he did with the message? Is it anywhere in the cottage?" No. "I suppose he took it with him?" Yes.

If he took it with him, it might have been found on his body. Perhaps it *had* been. Lieutenant Molo was not going to tell *her* anything. Well, but suppose it were not on the body. What would that show? He might just have thrown it away. Or . . . whoever killed him might have taken it back because it was evidence against him. Either way, it was necessary that she tell the police what she had learned. If they had found the message, it might still be of help to tell them how it had arrived. It was odd that Molo had not questioned Mrs. Cartwright about this. Perhaps they had not found a message. In that case, what was all that business about whether or not Mr. Ruz could write English? Had there been *another* message? Perhaps . . . to Barbara?

Useful or not, her duty was clear. The police would have to be told.

WHEN MRS. MOFFAT, ONE OF THE BLUE-HAIRED LADIES, came to take her turn with Mrs. Cartwright, Mrs. Wagstaff nodded reassuringly at the invalid and went off to tell the lieutenant her news and to send the wire to Anne Markham. It was hot and still in the garden. Nothing stirred, not even the two somnambulistic-looking policemen who had suddenly appeared at the ends of the garden watching . . . what? It was hard to imagine a sinister shadow creeping about under this bee-buzzing sunshine to enter some cottage, to attack someone. Hard . . . but after all, quite possible. Mrs. Wagstaff's skin twitched suddenly like a horse's beset by flies. It was hard to keep reminding herself that there actually *was* someone about who had drowned a girl and cut a man's heart out!

Neither Lieutenant Molo nor his little sergeant was in the hotel, and she came out again into the sinister sunlight to look over the garden.

"Madam!"

She turned sharply. The professor was sitting in the corner of the terrace with the bougainvillea vines draped half over him. He looked as though he were hiding.

"Are you hiding?" she asked.

He thrust his curly beard over his shoulder and looked for a moment at the terrace doors. "I had not been aware of it, but *yes,* I am hiding. The whole tour group is sitting about the bar, and if I hear Mrs. Gibson say once more that we are all going to be murdered in our beds, I shall take the knife to her myself!"

Her mouth stretched into her incongruous gamin grin. "That is a very dangerous kind of remark. If you recall *Habeas Indecorous,* a man was almost hanged when he was overheard saying something rather similar."

He shook his head irritably. "I can't see that it matters much whether I get hanged or murdered in my bed!"

She looked at him more soberly. "I have to send a wire for Mrs. Cartwright, but after that, perhaps we might go out for a walk. I should like to go up to Dr. Canning's dig to see what they are doing there."

He was up with alacrity. "I am your man!"

"Good. If you will meet me here in ten minutes, I shall be back. We should be able to go up and get back in time for tea."

"Tea!" His eyebrows flew up in indignation.

"Or the beverage of your choice."

"Quite!"

But it was not as simple a project as it seemed. After she had sent the wire, she rejoined Professor Michelson. He was wearing a white, floppy hat that concealed all but his beard.

"Good," she said approvingly. "It doesn't do to get careless in strange climates, either with food or sun or insects." She glanced down at her stout walking shoes complacently. "Or with snakes."

They went around the end of the building and started toward the road. A policeman in brown khaki stood at the gate.

"No," he said firmly, and he tightened his grip on the nightstick he was holding.

"I beg your pardon?" said Mrs. Wagstaff, towering over him.

"Nobody go from hacienda," he said, a shade nervously.

"Do you mean," said the professor, in a tone that must have curdled a good deal of student blood, "that we cannot go for a stroll?"

"Sor——ry. It are lieutenant's orders, sir."

Mrs. Wagstaff sighed gustily. "It is for our own good, he probably said." She turned at the crunch of footsteps on the path and they watched two uniformed men coming down the road toward them.

"Lieutenant," she called, "may we not go out for a walk? The professor and I thought we would like to visit the dig."

As she spoke, Susan came out on the front porch of the hotel.

"Perhaps Susan would like to go too," she added quickly. Susan had already been up there two or three times, but she was so much interested in archaeology that she was likely to want to go . . . not to mention that Brian was there. A sizable expedition, after all, might seem safer to Molo from two points of view. They could chaperone each other's conversation, and they could fight off attackers.

Lieutenant Molo's bronze face turned to look at Susan, who began to come down toward them. "It is a danger to wander around when a murderer is still at large," he said.

"Yes, of course. A very wise precaution, but in this case, with three of us . . ." She looked at Susan. "Wouldn't you like to go up to the dig with us?"

Susan, who had been looking hot and dispirited, suddenly perked up. She pushed her glossy black hair back from her face and smiled radiantly. "Oh, yes," she said. "I'd love to."

Lieutenant Molo watched her a moment. "Well," he said, "I am going up there myself to see Dr. Canning. If you wish to go, you may go with us." He looked at his little sergeant. "I think you will be safe with us."

"Oh, good!" Susan all but clapped her hands. She wore no makeup, but her pale skin was flushed with pleasure. She looked, Mrs. Wagstaff thought, very pretty indeed. She had an idea that the lieutenant thought so too. He was, she realized suddenly, quite a *young* man. Not that Susan's prettiness was likely to do the lieutenant much good. Susan's radiance was all for Brian Bothwell. Still, it didn't do any harm for a girl to notice that she is being admired. And Susan, noticing, glanced at Mrs. Wagstaff and gave her a tiny secret smile.

Mrs. Wagstaff's brows rose over her answering smile. How remarkable a little confidence was! As long as she crept about under Barbara's shadow Susan seemed a large, pale creature nobody paid any attention to. Not because that was what she *was,* but because it was what she *thought* she was. She had quite good features, a fine complexion, and a most attractive figure. Beside tiny Barbara, she probably had always felt horselike. But alone she was simply a big girl with the firm body of an athlete. All it needed to turn her into a beauty was her own realization that she *was* one. And the notion was beginning to dawn in her eyes. Now she, Elaine Wagstaff, had been a big girl too, and there was no denying that she had a heroic nose, but *she* had never worried much about her looks. She had early decided she was made for love and gaiety, and her conviction had brought her both. Men had rather quickly forgotten about her nose. It was all a matter of feeling at home in one's own skin and refusing to be humiliated about it. She looked down at her formidable bulk. Clearly she had passed the point of being anyone's sex kitten. Fortunately, that was no longer her goal. For now, she would settle for the freedom to follow her own curiosity, and for the pleasures of leadership.

She gestured the lieutenant aside and told him about Mr. Cartwright's message. His eyes were bright with interest.

"Why did she not tell *us* that?" he demanded.

"How? You never asked."

"Mmmnn."

"I take it you have not found the note?"

He frowned. "I thank you for your information," he said.

Why did the police always treat people like idiots, she wondered. Why did they never give one a straight answer.

He walked on in silence, thinking who knew what ingenious thoughts! A short way down the road, before the pyramid field, a dirt track twisted sideways into the underbrush. Lieutenant Molo plunged into it and the procession followed him like a miniature safari. The trees were thick with vines and flowering, parasitical plants Mrs. Wagstaff didn't recognize.

"Look," she said. "It's Tarzan country. Wouldn't you expect him to come swinging through the trees?"

"I should not be averse to having him on our side," said the professor. "A most useful man, as I recall!"

They wound their way along a level track that was like a tunnel of green.

"Watch for snakes," said the lieutenant solicitously to Susan.

She stopped abruptly. "Snakes?" she said, with a tremor in her voice.

Mrs. Wagstaff smiled down into her broad chin, Susan was not a timorous type. She was trying out her feminine wings on the lieutenant. High time!

"Not to worry." The brown, beaked face was masterful. "There are here many snakes, but we are too many. They will not attack."

He led the way, poking ahead of him with a stick. The low ground began to rise suddenly. It could not be called a hill, but there *was* some slight pressure on the backs of their calves. And then, startlingly, through the brush and trees, they saw the sky . . . the sky and a vast, grassy mountain. But not a mountain. When they emerged into the open, they saw that the mountain was an unnatural, steeply ·sloped hill rising straight up from the level ground. In front of it were four tents, and men were moving about in the dappled sunlight.

Faces turned as they emerged from the darkness of the trees. Most of the faces were brown. They were native workmen, some with wheelbarrows, some with curious, forklike tools they were using for clearing the vegetation that covered part of the mound. Halfway around the hillock, a tanned but definitely white, thin face turned toward them and a pair of glasses glinted in the sun. Brian Bothwell.

Susan suddenly tripped, and trying to catch herself, grabbed the lieutenant's arm. He made it quickly available and caught her expertly as she pitched forward. It certainly looked authentic, Mrs. Wagstaff thought approvingly. The girl could act.

Under the shade of a stretched piece of canvas, Dr. Canning was sitting. He didn't look up when they came toward him. He sat, bent slightly forward, his shock of white hair half concealing his face. He might have been reading.

"Dr. Canning," said the lieutenant, withdrawing his arm reluctantly from Susan. "If you will be so good. I would like to speak to you . . . about this terrible matter."

Dr. Canning looked up slowly. He was not reading. His face had a haggard, numb look . . . the look of a man who has been in solitary confinement for a long time. "Yes?" he said. "Yes?"

Brian Bothwell was suddenly beside them. "Can I help you?" he said. "Dr. Canning is . . . not very well." His face looked thinner than it had two days ago, and the muscles stood out on his jaw as though he were keeping his teeth clenched. It had been a bad week for him, Mrs. Wagstaff thought. And in addition, he had clearly had to take the problems of the dig pretty much into his own hands.

"I am perfectly well, Brian," said Dr. Canning, his brow furrowing. He looked at them all with a puzzled air. "There is nothing the matter with me. It is just that I do not wish to work just now." A twitch like a searing flame, fled across his face. "I have perhaps worked too much. If I had not . . . If I had been more . . . available, then nothing . . . then Barbara. . . ." He stopped, his face wrinkling into lines of sudden age.

"We always feel that way after a tragedy," said Mrs. Wagstaff. "But few things can really be prevented." She paused. These were the things one always said, but it was useless to say them, even if they were true. But she was wrong. Even the oldest clichés were sometimes useful. They made a comforting noise in the air, they pushed morbid thoughts away long enough for healing to take place.

"It is urgent," said the lieutenant formally, "that we have your help in finding the murderer. He has killed twice. We must stop this at once."

Dr. Canning's face looked empty of all caring. Mr. Cartwright was nothing to him.

"He should be hanged!" Mrs. Wagstaff's voice was sharp as a pistol report. "Barbara's murderer should be hanged!"

Bothwell's head jerked sharply toward her, his glasses flashing blindly. But the greatest effect of her remark was on Dr. Canning. His head rose like a striking snake's, his white mane of hair upthrust and his brown, veined hands in sudden fists.

"Yes! I will kill him myself!"

The lieutenant cast a startled glance at Mrs. Wagstaff, but he was quick to seize the opening. "We need to know," he said, "how the ancient sacrifices were conducted. Mr. Cartwright and your daughter . . . both were killed in most unusual ways . . . like the ancient sacrifices, I believe. I know of these, of course, but only in a general way."

"What do you want to know?" Dr. Canning's voice was as hard and arid as baked earth.

"How, exactly, were victims killed in the cenote? Were they drugged first? Were they tied? Were . . . virgins, only, thrown into the pool?"

Dr. Canning shivered slightly, but his voice was clear. "We do not know *exactly* how they were killed. There was almost surely a ceremony at the edge of the pool . . . in that stone chapel. Perhaps there were drugs. Probably copal was burned. We don't know if the victims were tied. If they were, the ropes had long disintegrated from the remains that have been dredged up."

"Copal," said Mrs. Wagstaff thoughtfully. She looked up to see Brian's blue eyes on her.

"Copal?" he said. He sounded startled.

"What is copal like," she asked. The lieutenant was about to say something impatient to her, but Bothwell broke in.

"It is a resin," he said. "A gumlike stuff, usually in a ball which is burned for its incense smoke." He seemed pleased to tell her. He was, she had heard, Dr. Canning's star pupil.

"There was copal there then," said Mrs. Wagstaff slowly.

Lieutenant Molo's great beak turned toward her. "Where? Where was there copal?"

"On the stones of that broken chapel, near the cenote."

"*We* saw none," said the lieutenant suspiciously.

"There wasn't much. It was sticky and stuck to my hand. And there was a funny smell."

"Why did you say nothing?"

"It didn't seem . . . significant. But if it *was* copal . . . then . . ."

"Whoever killed her *was* making a rite out of it!" Brian's eyes blazed at them from behind his glasses.

The sudden silence was like a pulsation, a reverberation in all their heads. Mrs. Wagstaff looked to see if she had upset Susan, but Susan had wandered off somewhere. Just as well for her not to hear this.

"But it doesn't make sense," said Dr. Canning harshly. "Why would anyone do it? Who would do such a mad thing?"

"Yes." Bothwell spoke quickly, as if his mind were leaping ahead on a new track. "Why kill someone in that way? It would have to be someone who knew those old rituals . . . someone who wanted to go back to them. A madman. A fanatic!"

Lieutenant Molo looked at him. "It is what I think also. Mr. Cartwright's death was clearly of this ritual nature. I wished to know if Miss Canning's death also followed such a pattern. It is not an ordinary man who would kill in this manner."

"I should hope not!" Susan's voice was shrill. She stood in the entrance to one of the tents, staring at the lieutenant.

Bothwell's head turned as if on a swivel. "What are you doing there?" His voice was sharp. "I told you no one is allowed in the artifacts tent!"

Her jaw tightened. There was a stubborn streak there, Mrs. Wagstaff saw with surprise. The girl had seemed so docile.

"I'm not touching anything," she said with some asperity.

"I can't have people messing up the finds!"

"Oh, I'm sorry, Brian. I didn't touch anything. I just wanted to . . ."

"Oh, never mind, Brian," said Dr. Canning wearily. "You needn't be such a watchdog. She won't hurt anything."

"Sorry, Susan. It's just that everything in there is in very carefully numbered sequence. If anything gets out of order . . ."

Lieutenant Molo broke in impatiently. "Dr. Canning, what of Mr. Cartwright's death? You saw his body. Was it exactly as in the ancient rituals?"

"Yes." His voice was bleak, but some light had come back into his eyes. "We can't tell you anything *exactly*. We don't know that much, but . . . yes, the method was to open the rib cage and rip out the heart. The heart *was*, we believe, put in a basin. Sometimes the body was subsequently dismembered and the pieces thrown from the top of the pyramid."

Susan shuddered, and moved closer to Mrs. Wagstaff. "What hateful, crazy people," she said a little wildly. "They must have been lunatics . . . cannibals!"

"Not cannibals," said Bothwell. He looked down at her head. His voice was thoughtful, almost musing. "They believed that the gods were all powerful . . . and that they had to be propitiated with blood sacrifices or they would destroy the world. If you really believe that, then a few sacrifices are perfectly logical."

"True," said the professor, "in the Mayan days. But done *now*, it merely suggests mania." He tilted his head up so he could see out under the brim of his floppy hat. "Are there any believers left?"

He addressed Dr. Canning, but Bothwell broke in. "Yes," he said. "There are descendants of the ancient Maya. They are called Lacandones. There are not many now and they live mostly near Lake Peten and in Chiapas. Some have migrated." He paused. "I have seen a few around here."

"Ay, yes," said the lieutenant. "The Lacandones. But they are harmless now. They are just simple people."

"Maybe," said Bothwell. "But they know the old rites . . . and sometimes they go into the jungle to old ruins and practice them."

"*Human* sacrifices?" The professor looked startled. He was used to bloody rites, but the ones he knew were always securely in the past, discussed in brown leather volumes with rotting covers.

Well, we don't know that. But there *are* Lacandones around," he repeated.

"Where? Who?" the lieutenant probed.

Brian shrugged lightly. "You can tell by the look. They look exactly like the faces on the stelae and the friezes. Like . . . Ruz, for instance."

"Señor Ruz is Lacandone?"

He shrugged again. "It is very likely."

A finger of cold walked down Mrs. Wagstaff's spine. Señor Ruz. A strange, angry man. A man who didn't like the Mayans described as bloodthirsty. A man who clearly despised the tourists he purported to serve. She thought of his metallic bronze face at the swimming pool as he talked to José. José! But they were related, the little maid had said. Uncle and nephew. So José, too, must be Lacandone! But he looked different. Some mixture in his blood? Some Spanish? But if he and Ruz were both Lacandone, what, precisely, did that prove? That they might still believe in blood sacrifice? What was it Ruz had said to José? Remember . . . remember who you *are!*

Should she mention that? Nobody else had heard that conversation. Was it important evidence? On the basis of that conversation, it was conceivable that the lieutenant would arrest José. So much could be explained by it. José had been humiliated by Barbara. He didn't understand American ideas of flirtation. Suppose, just suppose he were really Lacandone and *thought* in terms of ancient ritual. And there was Barbara, taunting his manhood. Perhaps he was even descended from priests! Could that be what Señor Ruz had meant? Remember who you are!

Her mouth opened to say something of all this, but Dr. Canning was talking . . . talking as forcefully and clearly as though he had come back to himself again, was regaining his forces and his ideas. "Nonsense!" he said. "The Lacandone are just remnants of an ancient people. There are only a few hundred left. They are completely primitive and their rites are simple, agricultural fertility ones. They burn copal in pots. They don't sacrifice people!"

Bothwell was shaking his head, but after all, thought Mrs. Wagstaff, Dr. Canning was the head archaeologist. Bothwell was hardly likely to know more than Dr. Canning. She held her peace.

The lieutenant nodded. "I have only one more question now. Did any of you send a message to Mr. Cartwright before his death . . . on the evening of his death?"

Dr. Canning looked blank. Brian Bothwell shook his head. "*We* hardly knew him," he said. "*Did* he get a message?" "So Mrs. Wagstaff says. Mrs. Cartwright told her so." The lieutenant paused. "*You* sent no message, Professor?" he asked suddenly, turning on Professor Michelson.

"*I?*" He had taken his hat off, and his caterpillar eyebrows shot up on his high pink forehead. "Why on earth should I?"

"That is what we would like to know," said Lieutenant Molo. "Why on earth anyone should. What was in that message?"

But no one answered.

MURDER IS BAD FOR TOURISM . . . AT LEAST BEFORE THE
murderer is caught. After that, tourists swarm about sites of violence, savoring streaks of blood, bullet-pocked stones or hanging-
trees. It always surprised Mrs. Wagstaff how strong the appetite for
violence was. In almost everyone. Herself, she knew ruefully, in-
cluded. What would a hockey game be without blood on the ice?
Weren't the best boxing matches the ones where someone got
knocked out or beaten into insensibility? Had anyone ever counted
the magazines of horror and gory death on the newsstands beside
the innocent Chiclets? Or the movies where the great moment was
an ice pick in someone's eye?

The tour group was restive. So was the hotel management. Since
the murderer was still at large, the reaction was still fear and avoid-
ance. The second tour group had been allowed to leave, but no new
groups or hotel guests were permitted to check in. Reservations
were being canceled. All this left their own group to rattle about in
the halls and lounges with very little to occupy them but speculation
and nerves. After dinner they clung together in the warm light of

the lounge. Mrs. Crummit refused to go from one room to the next unless someone went with her. "You never know," she quavered, "who might be in there!"

Since Mr. Cartwright's death, the women were looking with great suspicion at all the men.

"I don't believe any woman could have done *that*," said Mrs. Gibson with some satisfaction. "It must be a man!"

"Come now," said Professor Michelson, his eyebrows jerking upward humorously. "Women can be quite as murderous as men!"

"I doubt *that*," said Mrs. Gibson. "But anyway, it would certainly take a man's strength to cut out a heart."

Mrs. Crummit let out a little squeak. Whenever the murder was put into words like that, it seemed peculiarly pictorial.

"I don't deny it would be more likely," said the professor. "But I don't think only a man could have done it. Any strong woman could have managed it too. As long as he was unconscious, and she knew where to aim."

"Well," Mrs. Gibson's eye settled on Mrs. Wagstaff, "I suppose it's possible . . . but surely not probable."

Possible or merely probable, there was no doubt that most of them believed in a male murderer.

"If Barbara were carried to the cenote, it would have taken a man, no?" Mrs. Bernardi asked.

"Not necessarily," said Mrs. Wagstaff. "Barbara was so light, even *I* could have carried her."

"I *dare* say!" Mrs. Gibson drained the last of her martini and set it down with a thump.

"Oh Mrs. Gibson!" said Mrs. Bernardi in a shocked voice, and everyone wriggled uncomfortably.

"What I want to know," said Mrs. Moffatt, "is what the police are *doing*? I told that man everything I knew again today, but *that* isn't solving anything. Are we going to have to stay here forever?"

"One thing they do is watch," said Mrs. Bernardi. "Watch and not let us out."

"They are at all the entrances and exits," Mrs. Wagstaff conceded, "but I wouldn't say very effectually."

"They don't have enough men," said the professor.

"Quite so. There seems to be one stationed at the entrance to the pyramid field. And there is one at the end of the garden and one at the hotel entrance, but it would be quite simple to get out over the garden fence in any number of places."

"Oh, dear!" Mrs. Crummit looked both frightened and indignant. "If we can get out, anyone can get *in*. Oh, my!"

"We are all right as long as we stay close together," said Mrs. Moffatt, moving closer to the plump little man who was her husband and who had never been heard to say any more than "excuse me" to anyone.

Mrs. Wagstaff looked around. It was not the group she would have chosen as companions in a shipwreck, but it certainly seemed innocuous. She couldn't really imagine any of these people committing such murders. They were all small and elderly—except Susan. She looked at Susan. This evening she was wearing a little lipstick and she looked quite attractive. But she was . . . no denying it . . . a big, strong-looking girl. And as a student of physical education, she must know a good deal of anatomy. Mrs. Wagstaff sucked in her breath and held it. And there was also motive. Susan had clearly been jealous of Barbara. But why Mr. Cartwright? That made no sense. She glanced at her watch and let out her breath. Three minutes and fifty-five seconds. Not bad.

Well, now, the men. Of the men there were Mr. Gumbiner, Mr. Moffatt, the professor, José, and Señor Ruz. Mr. Gumbiner was not conceivably a murderer. As for Mr. Moffatt, even if he *were* a homicidal maniac, he didn't look as though he was ever out of his wife's sight long enough to buy cigarettes. The professor was obviously much more possible. He was small, but he had a man's muscles. Looking at his quirky eyebrows and his eyes cast humorously up at her, however, she couldn't take him as a serious prospect. She had a theory about criminals—violent criminals, that is. She thought that they were generally people without a sense of humor. Humor meant a sense of proportion. Nobody with a feeling for the absurdity of life could be capable of cutting out a man's heart. For that, you had to believe—with solemnity—in your own importance, to believe your rituals were important to the scheme of things. You had to be a fanatic. She had known a few fanatics . . . and without exception they had been humorless, frightening creatures.

A Mayan fanatic. Señor Ruz leaped to the mind. Or José. If, that is, you left out a village full of Mayan descendants, any one of whom might be crazed with hate toward the endless, damned tourists who had taken over their world. Mrs. Wagstaff was very glad that she *was* a tourist, instead of having to *endure* them. Not that they were as vile and brassy as popular fiction said. But just because they were *there*, walking around, poking in, peering at you, asking dumb questions, ruining the familiar atmosphere of home. She was, on occasion, grateful that the Minneapolis suburb where she lived had nothing that could conceivably attract a visitor from even as far away as Saint Paul.

She looked up to find Professor Michelson watching her attentively from across the table.

"That is a *very* brown study indeed," he said. "Does it contain any solutions?"

"No. Just questions. Actually, it's motive that bothers me. Method is clear enough."

"Oh? Getting those two to the site of the crime seems to me even more complicated."

"That's easy." She waved a large hand dismissingly. "Cartwright, we know, received a message . . . and went. It is quite likely, since murderers are repetitive in their techniques, that Barbara got one too . . . a message that probably sounded intriguing and romantic enough to get her to the pyramid field alone."

"And what would have gotten Cartwright out? You would think he would be suspicious after Barbara's death, unlikely to go to any secret meetings."

"Unless it was signed by . . . a woman? Mr. Cartwright was a big man and probably not easily intimidated."

"What woman? And what would she have said?"

Mrs. Wagstaff shrugged. "I would give a lot to know what was in that note. Something to make him curious? Something blackmailing? A plea for help?" She brooded. "What bothers me is the question of insanity. If it was a maniac, then ordinary motives don't apply. It could be any vagrant rage. If it was someone sane, the motive could be jealousy or hurt pride . . . but why, then, the maniacal *method*? They just don't fit together."

The professor nodded slowly. "It's like the Piltdown skull hoax, isn't it? The jaw and the brow could not come from one head."

"Just so. A good illustration." She stared into her drink. "What *is* insanity, after all?"

"Legally or socially? In perception or in action? Legally it's a state of mind where one doesn't recognize the import of one's acts and therefore can't be held responsible. Socially, one can be considered insane if one's acts simply don't conform to the culture's norms. One can be called insane if one's perceptions are off . . . if one sees dogs, for instance, that aren't there. Or one can be considered mad if one *does* something mad . . . hangs all day upside down from a tree . . . or cuts out somebody's heart!"

"Unless," she mused, "it's in one's tradition to hang from a tree or cut out a heart. For a Mayan, such a murder would be ritually correct, quite *sane*. And that means either José or Señor Ruz, if they are Lacandones. And José *was* quite infatuated with Barbara."

"Oh?" He eyed her sharply. "I didn't notice that. How do you know?"

She told him the incident at the swimming pool on their first night at Chichén, and added the odd confrontation between José and Señor Ruz.

He whistled softly. "Elaine, you've been withholding evidence."

She frowned. "No," she said. "I've been following my instinct. And that rejects José."

"He's a very good-looking young man. Could your instinct be affected by that? Actually, he makes more sense as the murderer than anyone. He is, let us say, Lacandone. He is infatuated, you say, with Barbara. She humiliates him. He gets her to come out with him, knocks her out, and then, because it would fit his religious background, he throws her in the cenote as a sacrifice. It makes a solid sum!"

"Too solid, maybe. The trouble is, Augustus, you didn't see her face when she came out of the pool. She was furious at him. I can't see her going out with him after that."

"But she *did* go out. We know *that*."

"But not to meet *him*." She stared at her empty glass. "We thought it was Cartwright. But how about Ruz? He's a strange man. And Barbara was intrigued. When she left, Susan said she seemed excited . . . not as if she were going to meet a man she already *had* wrapped around her finger. As if she were going to try something new . . . daring."

He looked at his own empty glass, thinking. Then the emptiness registered, and he crooked a finger at the bartender. "Yes. That isn't bad. Señor Ruz is also Lacandone. And he seems bitten with an interesting anger for his nephew. Mmmnn."

Mrs. Wagstaff stirred the new drink absently. "What worries me is the butler."

"The butler?"

"In books, it is always the butler . . . by which I mean the one least suspected by anyone. That's the whole theory of mystery writing. Introduce half a dozen people who have a motive. Bring in several red herrings who seem logical, and build up a case for each that the reader will think is plausible. Then knock down all the red herrings at the last moment and bring in the butler. And finally, spend a chapter or two explaining his motives and methods. Finis."

The white curls of the professor's beard blew out in the wind of his laughter. "You're ready to start writing your own now, Elaine. You have certainly got the system."

"I even have the title. *Around the Coroner*. How does that strike you?"

His eyebrows wriggled with amusement. "Perfect. Now you have only to plot it out. Cherchez the butler!"

She paused, her drink halfway to her mouth. "Cherchez the butler. Yes. Why not?"

He looked at her shrewdly. "All right, Elaine. Who is the butler?"

She smiled. "You must figure that out for yourself," she said sweetly. "Who is least likely?" With a creak and groan of corsets, she reared herself up from the table. "I am quite adequately inebriated for one night," she said. "I think I shall go home and meditate." She tapped her forehead. "The little gray cells. The little gray cells!"

SHE WAS ON HER WAY TO MEDITATE, BUT SHE STOPPED
in first to see how Mrs. Cartwright was getting on with her new
companion. The companion who came to the door was a little,
roly-poly brown woman in white with a beaming, gold-leaf smile,
who might have been twin to the maid who had picked up lunch. She
had, however, been sent by the lieutenant to take care of Mrs.
Cartwright's physical needs and also, Mrs. Wagstaff suspected, to
keep an eye on her visitors. A most unlikely female policeman . . .
if she was.

"I've wired your sister," Mrs. Wagstaff said. "She should be here
as soon as a plane can fly her."

Mrs. Cartwright's head wobbled slightly . . . or perhaps nodded.
Her gray eyes were shiny with tears. Relief, probably.

When she got out to the garden again, she glanced down the path
and saw that there was indeed a policeman near the hotel. But it was
true that the hotel was unpatrolled . . . they hadn't enough men, and
they seemed not to have walkie-talkies either. Remembering Mrs.

Crummit's remark that if people could get out, then others could get in, she paused near the policeman.

"Isn't there someone who could walk up and down the fence?" she asked. The man's brown face was utterly blank. "I mean," she went on, "you can't *see* from here if anyone gets over the fence." Nothing. His eyes just glittered at her nervously. Obviously he spoke no English. She thought of translating her remark into Spanish, but it seemed a mountainous effort. Never mind. She went on, extending her walk around the whole perimeter of the garden, peering through the bushes at the bar fence that encircled the enclave. You would get pretty scratched up if you tried, but clearly it would not be too difficult to enter or leave their bosky dell without being seen.

She walked over and stood looking at the pool for a while and thought about butlers. It wasn't, she had realized while she was talking to the professor, all nonsense and trickery. Sometimes the most unlikely people *did* commit crimes, and almost always they were described by friends and neighbors as pleasant, kindly, and quiet folk who had not been known to swat a fly heretofore. Mystery writers weren't quite such fools as they were often pictured. Even the quietest, nicest people did have hidden depths and emotional lives that could spell murder. She stood, almost hypnotized by the glimmer of light on the water, running through the butler possibilities. "No," she said once, and "yes" another time. She could hear the distant, pacing footsteps of one of the policemen, and there was some nameless thrashing in the bushes, but nobody disturbed her.

At last, with a shake of her head, she pulled her eyes away from the glinting pool and started back toward her cottage. She could hear a clatter of voices from the terrace of the hotel as the lounge party broke up, and then as she sat on the wooden bench of her little porch, she heard people dispersing to their cottages. She held her watch to the light of her window. Ten-thirty. They had all lingered late tonight, loath to separate and go home. She waited. Susan would be along soon, and she had things to ask her.

The voices stopped calling back and forth and the footsteps ceased, but Susan didn't appear. Perhaps, Mrs. Wagstaff thought, she was already in. Perhaps she had come in earlier, while she had been near the pool, and had gone to bed. She approached Susan's window. There was a tiny glimmer of light from the bathroom, but she could see no one. Quietly she knocked at the door and waited. Susan was probably in the bathroom preparing for bed. But if she was, she didn't come out. The line of light from the bathroom drew a finger across the floor, picking out a dropped slip, a stocking, a single blue mule.

Mrs. Wagstaff stood irresolutely for a moment, and then marched firmly off the porch and toward the hotel. If Susan were still in the lounge, she would find her and walk back with her.

But the lounge was empty. Only the bartender stood behind the bar washing up glasses. She walked down the hall, peered into the dining room and the small writing room. A single, small policeman sat on a straight chair by the front door. He spoke no English. Finally she went back to the bar. The boy was turning out the lights.

"Wait," she said sharply. "Will you tell me, please, if you have seen Miss Sutter? Susan Sutter?" The boy looked blank. "The young, dark girl," she said impatiently.

"Oh. Yes. She went a time ago."

"Was she alone? How long a time ago?"

"I don't know. Maybe half an hour? Maybe little more? I think . . . alone. Yes?"

She stared at him a moment, but she was scarcely seeing him. Instead she was seeing that finger of light in Susan's cottage, that surprising finger. Just suppose, she was thinking, just suppose that the murderer was *not* a maniac. What then?

She turned like a bull elephant and went out on the terrace. The garden was silent. She started rapidly down the path to her cottage. It was as still as when she had left it. She cupped her hands and stared through the glass of Susan's window. The finger of light had not moved. It pointed. A slip. A stocking. A blue mule. What was so surprising about that, she asked herself, but she knew the answer before she asked. Susan was a remarkably neat girl. Barbara might have left that mess on the floor, but Susan would not have. Unless . . . unless she were in a great hurry.

On the bedside table she could see a book and a scrap of paper and an ashtray. The paper was odd. Twisted into a tormented ribbon. But from here she could make out nothing too clearly. She went into her own room and got her sack. There was a trick she had known when she was a girl at college. Perhaps it would still work. She rummaged hurriedly and found her plastic library card. With this in hand, she went back to Susan's door. There were Yale locks on the doors . . . *old* Yale locks. She poked the plastic card in between the two sides of the lock and turned the knob. Now, if it were anything like her dormitory door, the lock should be pushed aside just far enough. She tried once, twice. Her hand was out of practice. But on the third try, it worked. The plastic card slid into place, and the door opened. She was in like a flash. Nothing inside looked unusual, except for the messiness of the place. The bathroom was full of spilled powder and an overwhelming smell of perfume where a bottle had been dropped on the tiles. She looked at the bedside table. Something charred lay in the ashtray, like burned paper. She took up the twist of paper beside it and brought it to the bathroom door to look at it. Untwisted, it showed only two words, written in pencil, and repeated three times. It was a woman's writing. Susan's writing, she guessed. But it was the words that suddenly galvanized Mrs. Wagstaff into action.

She dropped the paper and almost ran into the night. She had waited too long. What if she had waited too long? She stared down the long garden path toward the dim bulk of the hotel. There was that policeman. But he spoke no English, and there just wasn't time to explain. She thought of Barbara, and her heart battered in her chest.

Behind the cottage was a little, grassy glade that went almost up to the fence. It was one of the easier ways out, as she had observed earlier. She pushed aside the leaves of an oleander bush and heaved her great bulk somehow over the bar fence and into the tiny woods beyond. From there it was only a few yards to the road. It was black dark in the woods, and she tried not to think of snakes. All she could think of was time. There was no *time!* When she emerged on the road, she looked anxiously back. The hotel gate was a quarter of a mile back, and she couldn't see the man posted there. If he *was* there. And he didn't speak English. And there was no time. Susan had been gone almost an hour!

Down the black ribbon of road she went, walking solidly but rapidly, like a rhinoceros. She knew better than to try running. She would founder in a moment. But she could walk, and walk fast, for a very long time. Gerald had always envied her that.

Down the road she could see the dim glow of the street lamp by the pyramid field. Susan had to have come this way. The policeman would not have let her out, so he must not have seen her. She must have come over the fence . . . and where else was there to go?

But when she got closer, she saw that there was no one on guard at the entrance. No one. She had counted on Molo or his guards . . . *someone* to be here. And the gate yawned open and silent, and beyond there was just the ghostly glimmer of white temples and the black bulk of Kukulcan.

What was she doing here, silly old trout, she thought, anxiety and horror rising like bile in her throat. What could she do alone about Susan? About *anyone,* fat and feeble as she was! But it was only her frustration talking, her dread. She was fat, but she was not, nor had she ever been, feeble. And even while she thought so despairingly of herself, she was in motion. She strode across the great, dark field toward the processional road, a black cave in the trees. Faintly glimmering stood the pillars of the warriors, and the pale, scallop curve of the Chac Mool.

She stared toward it, her heart shuddering in her breast, but she could not see if there was anything there.

She never got closer to it. As she was passing the pyramid, she stopped short. Her nose rose like a pointer's, snuffing the warm night air. Something vague and sweet curled into her nostrils. She had a sensitive nose. It was not that large for nothing. And now it registered something strange to the general night air. A perfume, a smoke . . . something familiar. It took no more than a moment and the association came. Nothing assaults the memory so quickly as a smell. It was the same odor she had smelled on the day she found Barbara. That faint, sweet, smoky smell from the sticky resin on her fingers. Copal! Her heart began to beat in great, slow thuds. Copal. Nobody used copal any more. Not for any ordinary purpose. And Susan was missing, out here somewhere!

She stared up at the vast pyramid beside her. It loomed black as a mountain, and as silent. The only light was a faint shimmer of starlight caught on the iron chain that snaked up the great river of steps. Where did the smell come from? She walked quickly on toward the temple of the warriors, but the smell receded. It was there, by the pyramid of Kukulcan! She half ran back to the base again, her nose twitching with strained effort. Yes. Here it was strongest, right here. She strained upward into the darkness. Surely that was a light up near the top. A light, or perhaps just the glint of a star. It was too dim to make out with any certainty. But the smell was here, and with a twitch of horror her mind flashed back to the morning by the cenote, with the policeman carrying that grim white package that had been a lovely young girl.

It had to be here! She thought no more, but with a heaving effort, pulled herself up onto the first step and began to climb. If she were wrong, it would be too late to correct her mistake. But she had to try something . . . and the smell was clear. The chain was almost sticky-warm in her hands. Thank God she couldn't see down! She was not subject to vertigo, but she was not young any more, and the steps were so narrow she could barely put her large black dress shoes on them. The slope was so steep that her face almost touched the stone above as she climbed. It was all mad, and *she* was mad, too, to be out here in the Yucatán night alone, and panting up the side of this monstrous pile. But the smell was growing stronger. Surely she wasn't wrong about that! The sweetish smell mingled with the gritty dust of the steps, but it drew her onward. The climb was endless, and her heart banged against her huge bust almost hard enough to knock her down. But at last the chain drew her hands down. The end of the chain was fastened to the top step. Beyond it her groping hands could feel nothing but air.

How had it looked in daylight? What was up here? She could remember only an open stone platform with a small block of a temple on it . . . no railings, no chains, nothing to hold on to. If she let go the chain she would be standing on a space no more than two or three feet wide, with the great fall of steps below her. For a few seconds she held tight to the chain, motionless . . . but the smell was strong here, and there *was* a light, the smallest flicker, but it came from the little stone house just before her face.

With an effort of will, she rose to her full height, letting go the chain, and stepped up one last, unprotected step to the platform. Her hand pressed the grateful roughness of the stone wall of the temple and she looked down only once, into a well of blackness. Then she inched silently to the hole that was the doorway. From here the smell was as dense as smoke. It *was* smoke. Carefully she leaned against the wall and moved her head sideways until she could see into the small space where the ancient priests had sacrificed their captives to the gods.

Her breath rattled in her throat as she gazed. In the dim interior, on the altar, she could just make out a figure draped over the rock. An arm dangled, white and bare in the faint glow that came from a single flame . . . a dim wick in a round ball of resin, the copal. She was too late! Her great bulk shuddered as she made to hurl herself into the room . . . but she caught herself awkwardly before she had moved into the doorway. There was someone else in the room. A dark shadow moved from the corner toward the altar stone. A darkness came between her and the still, white figure, and then a dark arm upraised, holding something.

"No!" she cried out, a great organ note ripped from her throat. "Stop!" She glared wildly about for a stick, a weapon, anything. She had left her sack below, and the floor was bare earth. There was not even a stone loose in the room.

The black shadow gasped, and swung about. She heard, as if from a foggy distance, an answering cry from below, and a roaring sound like a vast, cosmic engine, but there was no time to listen or wonder. She reached down, scooped up the burning ball of copal, and threw it with all her strength . . . at that pale head. It hit with a hollow thud and a shower of sparks, and the man's hands flew to his face. Something clattered to the floor. He groped and started toward her. Breathless, she waited for no more. She backed out of the doorway precipitately and onto the narrow platform. The dark figure lurched after her, and away from Susan. She stared desperately behind her at the dark sweep of narrow steps, but she was too far from the chain to reach it.

"Wait!" she cried. But he did not wait. She fled heavily along the edge of the platform toward the chain, but he was after her, he was faster than she.

And then the sun flamed up. A great gout of light bloomed on the platform and caught him like a fly impaled on the wall. It lit up his eyes, shone on his pale hair, pinpointed the knife in his hand as though he had been flashed on a screen. The whole pyramid blazed white in the brilliant light, and on it in a line, hands linked, black figures were swarming up the steps.

Mrs. Wagstaff heard a voice cry "Elaine!" But she was too stunned by the light to think or connect the word with herself. She stood benumbed on the very edge of the platform, waiting to meet the charge of that wild shape, to be flung from the top.

But he, too, was stunned. His forward motion was checked, and when she sat suddenly on the top step, he tripped against her great bulk, tottered, lost himself, and fell, twisting and turning, thumping head over heels down the great flight with a scream that tore the balmy air.

The line of men caught him as he rolled on them, screaming and broken. Above, Mrs. Wagstaff lay against the rock of the temple, waiting for breath and life to come back to her. She breathed in five great yoga breaths. Susan, she thought then. Susan! Without looking down again, she moved along the platform to the door and went into the small stone room. The light, the miraculous light, shone into the place and struck Susan's black hair, cascading over the altar stone.

"Susan!" she said sharply. She looked at the girl's body. There seemed nothing wrong with it . . . no terrible gashes, no blood. Just that immobile figure, that limp hand. Mrs. Wagstaff leaned her head over and pressed her ear to the girl's chest. Slowly, flutteringly, the beat came to her ears. She was alive. Not well . . . but at least, alive.

"YOU'RE MAD!" SAID THE PROFESSOR INDIGNANTLY, helping her down the last steps of the pyramid. "Who do you think you are, Tarzan? Why didn't you call me . . . or call the police?"

"Well, Augustus, there just wasn't time. Susan had been missing too long." She gave a great, gusty, tired sigh. "And besides, I thought the police would be guarding the field, and I would find them."

"And so we were," said the lieutenant.

"Too far off to be of much use!" she said sharply.

He was sobered. "That is perhaps true, Mrs. Wagstaff. It may well be that you have saved Miss Sutter's life."

"*May?*" Professor Michelson's beard jutted forward fiercely.

"We were all here," Lieutenant Molo said. "We were watching!"

"*Where?* Where were you?" Mrs. Wagstaff's voice was wondering. "How did you all get here? What are *you* doing here, Augustus? I don't understand this great assemblage!"

"I went to look for you," said the professor. "In your cottage. But you weren't there. And neither was Susan."

"What did you want?" asked Mrs. Wagstaff curiously.

"I'd had an idea. You and your butlers! It occurred to me to wonder who it would be if it *were* the butler!"

"What are you speaking of? What butler?" Lieutenant Molo sounded bewildered. His parrot nose pecked at the air.

"It's just a joke," Mrs. Wagstaff said soothingly. "But tell me, lieutenant, where *were* you? Why didn't I see anyone?"

The lieutenant's nose dropped. "I was . . . on the road to the cenote."

"He was watching for Señor Ruz!" The professor's voice was derisive. "He had his searchlight truck parked in the bushes there, waiting for Ruz. He thought it was Ruz!"

She looked at the young man's face. Surely that was an embarassed flush on the bronze cheekbones. "So did I, for a while," she said kindly. "Only he seemed *too* likely. If Señor Ruz was going to kill someone, the last thing he would do, I should imagine, was to do it in Mayan rituals. Unless, of course, he was a mad fanatic. And I didn't think he was. Or rather, I began to wonder who it would be if it were not the obvious madman, but someone quite, quite sane."

They turned at a sound above them and stood in silence, watching two men coming delicately down the pyramid sideways, carrying Susan.

"Is she all right?" the professor asked.

"Yes, I think so. I think she was just knocked out. Like Barbara."

It was the second trip those two surefooted Yucatecs had made down those monstrous steps. The first had brought down the battered body of Brian Bothwell, his leg and his shoulder broken. He was still alive, still conscious, his pale blue eyes rolling in his agonized face. They had carried him to the searchlight truck and laid him flat on the floor.

"Thank God for that light!" said Mrs. Wagstaff fervently. "It came just in time, or I'd have been pushed off the top. How did you know I was up there?"

The professor held up her sack gravely. "I tripped over it on my way to get the lieutenant. Most timely!"

"Take her to the truck," said the lieutenant to his men. "We will take them both to the hospital at Mérida."

"I don't think she needs to go to the hospital," said Mrs. Wagstaff. "Certainly not near *him*."

The lieutenant shook his head impatiently. "It is necessary that a doctor see them both."

Susan, lying on the ground on a blanket, moaned suddenly. They watched her eyes open and stare blankly up at them.

"What? Why . . . why are you here? What's the matter?"

Well, thought Mrs. Wagstaff, at least that was better than "where am I."

"You're all right, my dear," she said. "Just relax. We'll tell you all about it shortly. How do you feel?"

She felt her head gingerly. "My head hurts. What's happened? Where's Brian?" She pressed one hand down on the blanket and sat up, her black hair falling in dishevelment on her shoulders.

"It is a long story," said the lieutenant. He reached down and helped her to stand. "Should you be standing?" he asked solicitously.

She gazed at him in surprise. "Yes, of course. I'm all right. Except for my head. Where is Brian?"

"He is . . . injured," said the lieutenant. "He is being taken to the hospital."

"Oh," she said. "What happened? Where is he? Can I see him?"

The lieutenant glanced uneasily at Mrs. Wagstaff. How do you tell a girl that her boyfriend has just tried to kill her, if she doesn't even suspect it?

"Susan," said Mrs. Wagstaff, "it has been a difficult evening, and the lieutenant thinks a doctor should see you. I will drive with you to the hospital and we will talk on the way." She drew the girl toward one of the two cars that stood in the field. The truck, its searchlight off now, started up and lurched toward the gate.

Lieutenant Molo slid into the driver's seat. He leaned back for a moment to speak to one of his men. "Take care of the copal . . . and the knife. I shall need them in the morning. Then go back to the village. I will see you in the morning."

The man nodded.

"What time is it?" Susan asked in a faint voice.

Mrs. Wagstaff looked at the luminous dial of her watch. It was incredible. It was only midnight.

"YOU DON'T UNDERSTAND. YOU DON'T UNDERSTAND!"
Brian's voice from the open door of the emergency room was des-
perate. "What difference did it make? She was *dead.* Don't you
understand? She was dead!"

Mrs. Wagstaff, waiting across the hall to take Susan home, shivered, listening. She was suddenly clammy cold and very tired. They
had splinted his leg, and the lieutenant had been in there for half
an hour now, questioning him. She couldn't hear Molo's words, but
Bothwell's answers streamed out the door like a river of anguish.

"What difference did it make? She came . . . to meet *Ruz,* and I
killed her. And then . . . I didn't know what to do. I thought of the
cenote. It seemed . . . logical. The *virgin* pool!" His voice was so
bitter that the hair quivered on the back of her neck.

Molo must have asked something else. "She *knew.*" Bothwell's
voice sounded strangled. "She knew the knife was gone. She *must*
have. She was always in that damn tent. And then it was back again.
She would have noticed. Don't you see?"

Molo's voice was a murmur.

"Don't! of *course* she knew. Or she would have, the minute she thought . . . or remembered. That damn girl!"

Susan, thought Mrs. Wagstaff tiredly. Poor child. All she was to him, all she had ever been, was a problem . . . someone who might have noticed that a knife had been taken from the artifacts tent . . . and then replaced. And the minute she had noticed, she would tell someone. She would become a bomb that would blow him sky-high. How obvious. Now. And the worst horror was that he was probably wrong. Even if she knew, she might well have stayed silent. The girl loved him. If she loved him enough to go out to meet him in that murder-ridden Chichén night, she surely loved him enough to protect him from suspicion. Love could be such a deadly weapon! It cut all ways.

"Don't you see? It doesn't matter *how*. If you're dead, the rest is . . . academic." It was the ghost of a laugh . . . a gurgle in his throat.

It was all cover-up. The whole thing. And if you accepted the premise, utterly sane. If you had to kill someone, then whatever you did to the corpse afterward didn't matter. It wasn't madness to kill Cartwright in that ghastly way. It was logical. It pointed the police away from *him*, the cool scientist. It turned them toward ritual. Madness. Lacandones.

Mrs. Wagstaff stared down at her knuckles. There was blood on them from the steps of Kukulcan.

"Please!" A new voice, sharp and authoritative, intruded on the dialogue. "This man must sleep now. Come back tomorrow." The doctor. He came out the door of the emergency room, all but pushing the lieutenant. The doctor was an elderly man, with gray hair and a whey-colored complexion. He looked tired.

"May I take Miss Sutter home now?" She asked him.

He ran his hands through his hair. "Yes. Go ahead. She is all right. A little bump on the head." He sent a nurse scurrying. Molo's little sergeant planted a chair outside the door of Bothwell's room. The lieutenant wrote rapidly in a light blue notebook. The bright, antiseptic lights of the hospital corridor shone again from the white tile floor. She felt vague and floating, like someone drunk . . . or awake too long. When Susan came down the hall with the nurse, she had to gather her senses together as though they were bits of shrapnel.

"We're going home," she said gently. Susan looked at her from huge dark eyes.

"I want to see Brian," she said. "He's hurt. They won't let me see him. Please *make* them." She was a child who believed Mrs. Wagstaff could do anything.

"It's too late. He's asleep. Come now, and tomorrow we'll see."

And then they were in a car, and someone in a uniform was driving them endlessly through the night, and there were more lights, and the dim garden, and blessedly, beds.

MRS. WAGSTAFF SLEPT. IF SHE HAD NOT COME QUITE SO close, she might have said that she slept like the dead. Her head pillowed on her broad forearm, she slept so totally that only the heave of her nightgown showed she was alive. When she woke at last, it was half past nine and someone was knocking softly, but persistently, at the cottage door.

She stared about, saw Susan still asleep on the other bed, heard the knock repeat itself, and swallowed hard. Mrs. Wagstaff was not one of those who said "Waa-aah—ah?" when suddenly disturbed. She reached for her robe, staggered to her feet quietly, and went to the door.

"Yes?" she said. The little police matron who had been with Mrs. Cartwright smiled goldenly and spread her hands in apology.

"I am sorry to wake," she said. "Lieutenant Molo has asked that everyone on the tour come, please, to the lounge at ten o'clock. I thought you would wish a little time for dressing."

"Yes. Thank you. I shall be there. Does he want to see Miss Sutter also? She has had a bad shock. Perhaps she should sleep a little longer."

The little brown woman looked doubtful. "He said all . . ."

"It's all right. I'm awake."

They turned to look back into the room. Susan was sitting up, her head leaning on one hand, her face white as paper.

"I'll get dressed . . . in a minute," she said.

"We'll see," said Mrs. Wagstaff firmly. "If she is well enough, we will come together. Otherwise, I shall come alone."

The little woman smiled again, nodded, and went away. They could hear her soft, persistent knock a short way down the path.

"I'm fine," Susan said, and thrust her bare feet outside the covers. Then she looked at them a moment, bent her head down over her knees and began to cry. "I'm . . . sor . . . ry," she gasped. "I'm . . . so . . . so . . . rry."

"No need," said Mrs. Wagstaff. "I can't think of anyone with a more legitimate reason for crying."

It was true. Last night Susan had been ill and shaken, but she had insisted on knowing what had happened until Mrs. Wagstaff had decided it would affect her about equally to tell her the truth or to keep silent. She had not, at first, understood. Then she had not believed. At last she had both believed and understood, but she had been so numb with shock that she had simply taken the sleeping pill offered her when she got back from the hospital, and passed out at once.

It was not a story for a young girl to wake up to all over again. But it was there, and there was no glossing it over. It is never possible, Mrs. Wagstaff thought sadly, to hide from anyone very long that life is a painful affair.

She sat down beside the girl and put her arm about her shoulder. Susan pushed her head into Mrs. Wagstaff's neck and sobbed until she began to hiccup. "It's . . . true . . . isn't it?" she said at last, "about . . . Brian?" Her face was wet with tears, but she was quieting. "He *did* try to . . . *kill* me?"

"I'm afraid so," Mrs Wagstaff said.

"But why? I don't understand *why?* Am I *that* horrible?"

"It is *he* that is horrible."

"But he was so ... so *sweet* to me. He said he wanted to see me alone. He wrote that he *needed* to see me and he'd meet me just over the fence behind the cottage."

"And did he?"

"Yes! He was right there, waiting for me!" Her eyes filled again. "How could he do that when he wanted to kill me?" She gave one last hiccup and sat suddenly back, staring at Mrs. Wagstaff. "Was he ... crazy?"

"I don't know. He certainly did some crazy things. I suppose one could say the ancient Maya were mad, by our standards. All that blood and slaughter. But it seemed perfectly logical to them. And maybe ... at last ... to *him*. He'd worked so long with Mayan ideas. You remember, he said something like that at the dig ... that they were quite logical. I suppose what he was doing seemed quite logical to *him* too."

"But *why?* I would never hurt him. Why did he want to kill *me?*"

"I think," said Mrs. Wagstaff gently, "that after Barbara's murder, the rest was self-defense. A cover-up. He thought you and Mr. Cartwright knew about him, that you could betray him."

"But I didn't know *anything!*" She gazed at Mrs. Wagstaff wretchedly. "He said he needed me. He said it was all a mistake about Barbara. She never meant anything to him really. He said it was me all along, but he hadn't realized ..." Her voice trailed off.

"Did he write this to you?"

She nodded dumbly.

"And you burned the note?" That char in the ashtray!

"He asked me to."

Mrs. Wagstaff sighed. Love! The poor child would do whatever he said. Burn evidence. Go out into the murderous night. Walk to the field ... climb that awful pyramid!

"Why did you climb Kukulcan?"

"He said ..." She lowered her head. In the clear morning light it began to seem to her, too, so foolish ... so credulous. "He said it was so ... lovely up there when the moon came up. He wanted to ... show me."

Mrs. Wagstaff nodded. Yes. She had known, or at least guessed something like that . . . ever since she had seen that twist of paper on Susan's bedside table. The paper had had only two words on it, repeated three times over. Susan Bothwell, it had said. Susan Bothwell. Susan Bothwell. And Susan was missing. And she, Mrs. Wagstaff, didn't believe that Brian Bothwell cared anything about Susan Sutter. So something had happened. Something had happened to make Susan think he cared. Something had suggested to her the lovely fantasy of being Susan Bothwell . . . perhaps a piece of burnt paper? And so Susan had gone off into the night.

"Come," she said firmly. "Go wash your face and put on some clothes. There must be some answers that the lieutenant has for us."

Susan shuddered, but she got up and made her way to the little bathroom.

When they got to the lounge, it was full. The members of the tour were all there, some of them still wiping the breakfast eggs off their mouths.

"Well," said Mrs. Gibson when she saw them, "the heroine of the evening!"

"You were wonderful," Mrs. Crummit fluttered. "How did you have the nerve to climb way up on that pyramid . . . in the *dark?*"

"It was easier in the dark," said Mrs. Wagstaff. José set a chair for her with his usual grace, and the professor pushed his for Susan. Near the door to the lobby, a tall, fair woman with a curly bob stood with her hands firmly on the handles of Mrs. Cartwright's wheelchair. Mrs. Cartwright's eyes were so alert that it almost seemed that she would begin, suddenly, to speak.

"It's her sister," the professor whispered in her ear. "She just arrived this morning. She looks . . . *devoted.*"

"Ah. That's good. She deserves *some* luck." She looked pityingly at the invalid. Everybody on God's green earth needed *some* luck just to get through life. There was no accounting for the crazy fact that some people seemed to get an inordinate amount of it . . . and some people none. And whatever they said in church, it was chilly comfort to have only pie in the sky to look forward to.

There was a rustle at the door, and Lieutenant Molo came in with

Dr. Canning and Señor Ruz. Dr. Canning was shaking his head in angry bewilderment. "I can't believe it," he said. "He's as sane as you or I!"

"But Doctor, I did not say that he was not." The lieutenant looked up at him. "It would perhaps be better for all if he were *not.*"

Dr. Canning stared at him.

"Mania," said the lieutenant, "is its own excuse. At least that is so in the law. If, as you say, he is sane, then there is no excuse . . . in the law."

"But his work . . . he went on working, so *well.* I don't see . . ."

"That is because he was not at all mad in the usual sense. And he *had* to work well. He had to seem particularly . . . rational . . . in every way. Yes."

"Lieutenant," said Mrs. Gibson. "What is it all about? What has happened, *exactly,* and what are you going to do about us? Are we allowed to go now?" She looked crankier than ever. She would have preferred, Mrs. Wagstaff thought, for Susan to have turned out killer than victim. Victims got so much attention.

Lieutenant Molo held up his hand to stem the flood of questions that immediately broke out on all sides.

"Please," he said. "It is all over now. You will be allowed to leave very shortly. But I must take depositions from everyone . . . and I must ask that a couple of you stay an extra day or two."

"If it's all over, why do we have to stay?" asked Mrs. Gibson belligerently.

"Not you, my good lady. You are free to go."

Mrs. Gibson looked as if a chair had been pulled out from under her. "Well," she said. "Well! I think at least you ought to tell us what has happened. What did he do it for?" She looked around at them all triumphantly. "You know," she said, "I never trusted that young man! He was just too mealymouthed. The quiet type. That's just the kind that are all on fire *inside!*"

"That's quite true," Mrs. Wagstaff murmured, but Molo heard her.

"Mrs. Wagstaff," he said, "I must ask that *you* stay. It is fortunate that you *were* there . . . but I should like to ask just *how* and *why* you were on Kukulcan last night."

"Lieutenant!" Susan's voice was firm and clear.

"Miss Sutter?" The lieutenant's eyes lit up unmistakably. Unmistakably even to Susan, whose pale face grew suddenly pink.

"What has happened to . . . Mr. Bothwell?"

"He is all right. He is in the hospital . . . under guard. He has confessed."

"To . . . everything?" Mrs. Crummit breathed.

"To the murders of Miss Canning and Mr. Cartwright, and to the attempt on Miss Sutter's life. Yes."

"Ooo-oh," said Mrs. Crummit, her crumpled-petal face horrified, but fascinated. She had been writing one of her huge postcards to her daughter when the lieutenant came in, and it dangled now like some great, colorful parakeet in her hand. She looked at the few lines she had written, and then back at the lieutenant. "Will you tell us about it, please? I'm sure my daughter will be so interested!"

Lieutenant Molo drew himself up. His tiny assistant followed suit in an unconscious parody of his superior.

"I am sorry," he said, "but I cannot discuss details of what will shortly be a case for the criminal court." He looked at their curious, frustrated faces. "Of course," he said, "it is your right to speculate." He glanced at Mrs. Wagstaff. "I should guess that one of your number knows a good deal about the matter." He paused. "Now, if you will come in one by one to the office next door, I will take down your statements, and then you will be free to go."

He took Susan away with him first, holding her elbow and bowing like a brown, clockwork figure out of chivalric times. Dr. Canning accompanied them. The minute the door closed behind them, the dam broke.

"What happened?"

"Why didn't anybody call us last night?"

"Why did he do it?"

"Is he crazy?"

"Will he be put in an asylum?"

"What *were* you doing up there, Mrs. Wagstaff?"

Mrs. Gibson raised her hand like a general reviewing troops. "Wait a minute," she said loudly. "I think we're entitled . . . at *least* . . . to know what went on on *our* tour." She turned on Mrs. Wagstaff. "I think it's time you told us everything you know. Why, we could *all* have been murdered in our beds!"

Someone gave a hollow groan. Almost certainly the professor. Mrs. Wagstaff's urchin grin enlarged to cover her face.

"*I* don't think it's very funny that we should have been subjected to murder and police brutality on a *first-class tour,*" said Mrs. Gibson angrily.

Mrs. Wagstaff settled herself comfortably on a pale blue loveseat. "I'll be glad to tell you what I know," she said, "though, as Lieutenant Molo said, much of it is sheer speculation." She glanced at Professor Michelson. "I shall use the professor as a consultant. He is a literary expert on criminal practice."

Professor Michelson's curly brows flew up and down rapidly. He looked startled . . . but gratified.

"What *I* want to know," Mrs. Gibson said sharply, "is why that monster killed Barbara in the first place!"

"I think," said Mrs. Bernardi softly, "maybe because he loved her?"

"Well, *that's* a great reason!" said Mrs. Gibson.

"But quite true, I believe," said Mrs. Wagstaff. "He was quite besottedly in love with Barbara. And she was not an easy person to love."

"*I'll* say," said Mrs. Gibson.

"What I mean," said Mrs. Wagstaff calmly, "was that she was unwilling to tie herself to any one man when the world was so full of . . . potential . . . in that direction. The trouble is—" she sighed —"people are so possessive. Men are so often unwilling to accept *part* of a girl's attention. Mr. Bothwell was unwilling."

"How about Cartwright? He was kind of interested too, wasn't he?"

There was a sudden, protective flurry of movement near Mrs. Cartwright's chair. The tall, blonde woman made as if to move the chair out of the room, but Mrs. Cartwright gave a low, moaning cry, and her hands tensed on the chair arm.

"I think," Mrs. Wagstaff said, "Mrs. Cartwright would like to know the whole story."

The clawlike fingers relaxed, and the gray eyes closed and opened rapidly.

"Yes. Well, Bothwell wanted Barbara all to himself, and he considered himself engaged to her. He had given her a ring. But she felt quite unbound. And she . . . flirted . . . with other men quite openly." She glanced at José. He stood stiffly against the wall, his brown eyes still on her face.

"You mean he killed Mr. Cartwright from jealousy?" Mrs. Bernardi breathed.

"It seem possible . . . but actually, I think not. I think, after Barbara, it was all a matter of covering his tracks. But Barbara's murder was a kind of test and retribution. He tested her to see if she was faithful to him . . . and when she failed the test . . . he killed her."

"What . . . kind of test?" asked Mrs. Moffatt.

"He sent Barbara a message asking her to meet him at the pyramid in the evening . . . and he signed another name to the message."

"Whose name?"

Mrs. Wagstaff looked around the roomful of attentive faces. "I don't know," she said, "I have not seen it . . . but I think, perhaps, Señor Ruz's."

Señor Ruz's face was a study in mahogany.

"Why *him?*" demanded Mrs. Gibson.

"Because, I believe, Barbara seemed to find him . . . interesting. And because he wanted to see if she would possibly respond to someone she knew hardly at all. So he signed Ruz's name to the note, and then he went himself to the pyramid and waited."

"How do you know that?" demanded Mrs. Gibson.

"I don't know it for certain. But Susan described Barbara that evening as coming back from her date with Bothwell, dressing herself afresh, and going out again, with a considerable air of . . . mystery."

Señor Ruz suddenly spoke. It was like the great stone face coming to life. "That is good thought," he said. "The paper was found on her body. It asked that she burn it, but she did not." His lips thinned. "It *was* my name on it. I told Lieutenant Molo that I did not write it. I do not think he believed me!"

Mrs. Wagstaff looked at his sardonic expression and nodded. "Well, then, Barbara went to the field and there she must have met, not Señor Ruz but Bothwell. I don't suppose we will know exactly what happened then, but he must have gotten enraged and struck her. Knocked her out. And then he had the brilliant idea of throwing her into the pool." She looked thoughtful. "Probably he found the note in her pocket and thought it would be useful . . . since she hadn't burnt it . . . to leave it there and let it point to Señor Ruz . . . especially if he turned her death into a kind of Mayan sacrifice."

"You mean he set it *up* that way? Like a play?" Mrs. Bernardi looked breathless.

"I think so. That was the whole problem in this affair. The method of the murders was so bizarre. After all, it is relatively easy to kill someone. Bothwell might even have killed her by his blow. But why all the Mayan elaboration, I keep asking myself. And there are only two possible answers."

"Two?"

"Quite," said the professor. "Either the killer *is* a Mayan fanatic . . . or someone wants it *assumed* that he is."

Mrs. Wagstaff nodded like a pleased Great Dane. "It must have seemed to him a great way of distracting attention from himself. After all, he appeared to be a perfectly normal, sane scientist. Who would expect him to do such a mad thing?" She leaned back and murmured to the professor "a perfect butler!"

"I didn't suspect him myself," she went on modestly—"although I did rather wonder why he seemed so anxious to tell us that Señor Ruz and his nephew José were Lacandones, and that the Lacandones had inherited all that was left of the ancient Mayan religion."

"You mean," Mrs. Crummit's voice shook, "they still sacrifice people?"

"Certainly not!" José's liquid brown eyes were indignant. "There is more to our religion than blood sacrifice."

"Oh. Oh, I *am* sorry. I didn't mean *you* . . . I'm . . . I meant . . ."

"Of course you didn't," Mrs. Wagstaff said powerfully. She was not about to let her tale get thinned by interruptions. "Of course, if Señor Ruz were to be a good suspect, it did no harm to suggest that he was a descendant of people who *did* make such sacrifices. I should rather guess that Brian elaborated on the idea after he had killed Barbara. That copal incense I smelled. He might well have burned that in the cenote temple as part of his suggestion of a ritual death. After all, he had all night, and he would certainly have known where to get some copal."

Señor Ruz was shaking his head. "Not so," he said. "I do not kill any persons, but it was *my* copal." His heavy-lidded eyes looked out at them as though he were a stele carving. "We *are* Lacandone," he said, his voice heavy with the power and pride of centuries. "We are of the priest caste of the ancients, and we do still honor our god at the sacred cenote. It is so."

Mrs. Wagstaff was momentarily dismayed, but almost at once her eyes sparkled with interest, and she began to nod. "Yes," she exclaimed. "I see. Barbara's death was not ritually planned, except that she was thrown in the cenote. It was only later, when he had to kill again, that he thought to make use of the ritual forms. They were just . . ."

"Red herrings," the professor completed her thought.

"Exactly!"

"Well," said Mrs. Gibson discontentedly, "that's all very well, but I still don't see why on earth he had to go and kill poor Mr. Cartwright. What had *he* done?"

"It was not what he had done, I think," she said slowly, "as perhaps what he had seen." She turned to the professor. "Augustus, you saw Mr. Cartwright that night. What was he doing?"

"He came out of the hotel rather fast and went down the road toward the pyramid field. I thought he seemed in a hurry, and he seemed to be a bit . . . furtive. But I didn't think much of it. I went in another direction."

"So what does *that* show?" asked Mrs. Gibson.

"It shows, I believe, that Mr. Cartwright had perhaps seen Barbara go off down the road, and he was following her." Mrs. Wagstaff's eyes on Mrs. Cartwright were not pitying or sentimental. She did not believe that Mrs. Cartwright's feeling for her husband was . . . any longer . . . love.

"I would guess—and this is pure speculation—that Mr. Cartwright went after her and paused near the gate to see what she was up to. He probably guessed she was going to meet someone. She didn't go about alone very often. And the someone was Bothwell."

"You mean, they *saw* each other?"

Mrs. Wagstaff's brow furrowed like a bloodhound's. "I don't know. From the results, I would think Bothwell saw Mr. Cartwright, but not vice versa."

"If I may," said Professor Michelson in his most expository schoolroom manner. "There was a lamp near the road. Bothwell could see Cartwright standing there, but he himself was in the dark, near the pyramid. Probably Cartwright couldn't see who it was. I've tried myself. You can't see much across that field in the evening."

"But I don't suppose Mr. Bothwell realized that. For the moment, perhaps just after he'd struck Barbara, he saw Cartwright looking toward him. He must have thought Cartwright could see *him* as well as he could see Cartwright. And so Mr. Cartwright had to be . . . disposed of."

"And quickly," the professor added, "before he could talk to the police. They made a mistake not to question everyone at once!"

"Yes." Mrs. Wagstaff looked suddenly inspired. "That was what Mr. Cartwright was doing when I saw him near the pyramid that afternoon. I thought he was looking for something he had dropped, something that would incriminate him." She threw a quick glance at Mrs. Cartwright. "But what he was really doing was looking for some clue to who the man was that Barbara had met there. If he could tell that, he would know the murderer!"

"But how did that Bothwell get Mr. Cartwright to come out that night. Why *would* he? Wild horses couldn't have made *me!*" Mrs. Gibson looked tensed against those wild horses.

"I don't know for sure, but he *did* get a message slipped under his door."

"Murderers," said the professor didactically, "tend to repeat a successful tactic. Like students! He must have sent a note asking for a meeting to tell him something urgent . . . or to ask advice."

"Bothwell?"

"Probably not signed so," said Mrs. Wagstaff. "He had, before, signed another name. Perhaps this time, he signed . . . Susan? Someone Mr. Cartwright would not be afraid of."

"Well, maybe." Mrs. Gibson was skeptical. Her face was very red, and her wattles shook like a rooster's. "But Mr. Cartwright was a big man . . . bigger than that Bothwell fellow. How could he kill him like that?"

"It's very easy to kill someone who doesn't expect to be attacked," said Mrs. Wagstaff. "Surprise is everything. If he went into the field to meet someone—perhaps right to the Chac Mool where he was found—and especially if he thought it was to meet a girl—he would be completely unsuspecting. Particularly because it would not have occurred to him that the murderer had seen *him* the previous night. After all, *he* had not seen the murderer. It was the same error as Bothwell's . . . but in reverse. Each one would have thought the other could have seen what *he* saw. In the one case, Bothwell would have thought Cartwright would have seen him. In the other, Cartwright would have thought the murderer had *not* seen *him*." Mrs. Wagstaff paused, her eyes alight with conviction. "A sort of ostrich situation. If one's head is in the sand, one forgets that one's body is showing."

"So what happened?"

"Bothwell must have knocked him out. It would be easy to step out from behind one of those pillars at the temple of the warriors and hit him over the head. After that, there would be no trouble with the rest of the . . . program. Another "ritual" murder, another finger pointing at a maniacal fanatic."

A hoarse noise came from Señor Ruz's throat. There was a malignant gleam to his black eyes. *"I!"* he said.

"Quite so." Mrs. Wagstaff nodded. "Who more likely?"

"Why not me?" demanded José suddenly. "Surely I was just as good a candidate!"

"Almost." Mrs. Wagstaff smiled at him. He *was* a very handsome young man. "But you have worked as a guide for some time. You are so used to tourists . . . so *like* them . . . that it is less easy to associate you with ancient rituals." She looked at him a moment. "I beg your pardon," she said. "I didn't mean you were really *like* tourists. That was a gratuitous insult. I just meant you were closer in manner and training."

"Huh!" Mrs. Gibson was explosive. "I don't see why it's an insult to be a tourist!"

Mrs. Wagstaff sighed. "Not if you *are* one, of course."

The door opened and Susan and the lieutenant came in. His hand hovered under her arm protectively, but she needed no help. Her head was up and her back as straight as a die. Thank God for pride, thought Mrs. Wagstaff, watching her. It was bad enough for a girl to be jilted by the man of her choice. It was infinitely worse to be murderously attacked by someone you thought loved you. Yet here she was, upheld by some stoic refusal to show pain. Odd that pride was considered such a dire sin in the Bible—the worst sin of all. It was often so helpful.

The lieutenant's gutteral voice was as soft as a mourning dove's. "Miss Sutter," he said. "You need not wait any longer. If you wish to rest . . ."

She looked at him. They were of a height. But she must have seen something in his eyes, the sort of expression that makes a woman feel valuable. She smiled at him, ever so faintly.

"Thank you," she said. "I think I will go and pack. I will be staying with my uncle for a few days."

"I will come and help you," said Mrs. Wagstaff.

"I will see you at lunch, Elaine," said the professor. "I have an idea for a literary collaboration that might be of interest."

"Mm-nn-mm," she said, nodding. "Minneapolis has been getting a little dull . . ." She took Susan's arm.

"Hey, wait a minute," began Mrs. Gibson, but the two women were already out on the terrace.

"Let them go," said the professor. He sat down in a carved,

Spanish chair and regarded them all like a white-bearded Mephisto-pheles. "If there is anything else you want to know, just ask me!"

Luncheon in the shade of the bougainvillea vines was almost over. They sat with their coffee and looked benignly at the sunny garden.

Mrs. Wagstaff, warm and relaxed, drew in a deep breath and held it. Maybe it was the sun, perhaps a good night's sleep. Whatever it was, when she looked at her watch, she let out her breath in a great gust of delight. "Four minutes," she said. She could hold her breath as long as a pearl diver—long enough to open a car door under water.

"Well, congratulations," said the professor, who had been let in on her effort one day when she had turned alarmingly blue. "But to get back to our case, Bothwell doesn't fit your butler theory."

"Oh?" Sun, food, and triumph had made her a little sleepy.

"Of course not. The least likely murderer was not Bothwell at all. It was . . . Mrs. Cartwright!"

Her corsets creaked and groaned with her laughter.

"Don't laugh! The poor invalid who is *not* an invalid. She gets out in the night and does her dastardly deeds . . . and, of course, nobody ever suspects!" His furry eyebrows flew up his forehead, leaving his eyes naked and innocent. "She was the obvious butler!"

"Augustus, you have what may be a fatal flaw in a literary col-laborator."

"Oh?"

"You read too many detective stories!"